I Is Another

ELISABETH RUSSELL TAYLOR

I IS ANOTHER

PETER OWEN
London & Chester Springs PA

PETER OWEN PUBLISHERS
73 Kenway Road London SW5 0RE
Peter Owen books are distributed in the USA by
Dufour Editions Inc. Chester Springs PA 19425–0007

First published in Great Britain 1995
© Elisabeth Russell Taylor 1995

ISBN 0–7206–0959–3

A catalogue reference for this book is available
from the British Library

Printed and made in Great Britain by
Biddles of Guildford and King's Lynn

To Tom who told me that life is not
a feast but a predicament

Madness is nature's last resort against anxiety.

Schopenhauer

This book has been written with the assistance of a grant from the Arts Council. I should like to thank the Arts Council for its generosity.

E.R.T

PART ONE

Canst thou not minister to a mind diseased,
Pluck from the memory a rooted sorrow,
Raze out the written troubles of the brain,
And with some sweet oblivious antidote
Cleanse the stuff'd bosom of that perilous stuff
Which weighs upon the heart?

Shakespeare, Macbeth, V. iii

I was not inclined to stretch out on the couch as Dr Auerbach indicated that I should. But since he made it clear that I was not to sit at the table where his papers lay exposed, I sensed I had no option. I felt deep unease. I was laying myself out on an operating-table.

'So you are having trouble sleeping.'

I had agreed to keep the appointment my wife Sabine had made for me because I always tried to accommodate her. However, I did not imagine that mere conversation would ease the sleeplessness that strong medication had failed to cure. In the event, neither the doctor nor his consulting-room gave me confidence. The doctor was curt, his room so sparsely furnished it might have been a cell.

I have never felt the need to speak about myself. There is very little to say and I am frightened it might make me start inventing things, or that things of which I am unconscious might emerge. I am a chef. That is, more accurately, I was a chef. A good one. A celebrated one. The only one in the country to have earned four stars. But my story does not begin with me. Everything that happened to me was precipitated by my wife. This is not to blame her, I must emphasize the point. Without the support of Sabine, not to mention her thoughtfulness and enthusiasm, my whole adult life would probably have unfurled without incident. It would have been featureless.

I would have remained in obscurity, for all time a commis.

Sabine is a remarkable woman, perhaps too remarkable for someone like me. I am ordinary, an ordinary man. In Sabine's opinion, to be ordinary is the greatest crime of all. ('Stupifyingly mediocre' is one of Sabine's favourite and most frequent invectives.) I made a name for myself as a chef, not as a man. I would never have made a name for myself as a human being. This is something, a subtlety you might call it, that Sabine could not take on board. She is constitutionally unable to admit the distinction. For her it is a man's calling and the honour he bestows upon it is what betokens his worth. She looks to the tip of the iceberg and draws her view from there.

It is a credit to her impeccable taste and management (and her confidence in me) that our restaurant, Les Coteaux, was the sole establishment in the country to boast four stars. Four stars assured us of celebrity. But I never did accept this for myself. Three hundred years ago and my work would have gone unremarked. In those days chefs were not only great artists, they were considerable men. I know this for a fact; I have read prodigiously on the subject. I trod in the footsteps of the great chefs of the past; I followed their advice, their planning and their recipes. My talent was to interpret their creativity intelligently. I felt justified in this practice on the grounds that the public go to listen to Brendel as much as they go to hear the composer he is interpreting. I myself aimed to be the executant *par excellence* of my masters. It was only when Sabine suggested, nay insisted, I invent dishes of my own that my trouble started. As I have said, I never wanted personal celebrity. I wanted the best restaurant in London dedicated to the traditions of *la grande cuisine française*. It was the food of my masters that I wished celebrated. I have never liked being singled out for attention. I cannot withstand adulation or vilification. This

14

accounts for why I always kept completely apart from our customers. My aim was anonymity.

Sabine's respect and admiration are reserved for the artist. It may be all right for men with private means, who live alone without responsibilities, to be artists, but for the likes of me with my background it would have been a practical impossibility, I thought. Nor did I see Sabine dressing herself from charity shops, living in a garret with a one-bar electric heater and electric ring, eating the sweepings from the Saturday fruit and vegetable market in the New End Road. However, I was resolved never to sacrifice my craft to commercial consideration. I know where to draw the line.

For those who provided us with our living, lesser royalty, senior civil servants, bishops, bankers and worse, Sabine had nothing but contempt. Had I observed, she inquired, how consideration is given to various occupations only in inverse proportion to their usefulness? How many times did I heard her purr down the telephone 'I am so sorry, we are fully booked for the next four weeks' and observe her satisfaction. When she could offer the caller a table, she would declare *couvert* for four or six, and thus dictate to the customer how many diners must be brought along to accommodate Les Coteaux. Then her cup overflowed. She pronounced her decrees with blameless courtesy. In her solicitous, mellifluous French accent, she concealed from our clientele what she revealed to me: her unequivocal, scornful judgement of the Establishment. To make a member wait on her convenience to dine at Les Coteaux provided my wife with an almost sexual frisson.

She referred to our customers as *les champignons*, bred on dung, the waste from good ideas that benefit only the few. (Stupifyingly mediocre!) The system is corrupt, she said, and men such as our customers use it for their own

15

aims. She had faultless recollection of names and faces. In addition to which, she collected books and magazines and cut out items from the newspapers about the privileged and powerful. She knew intimate details about their finances, their liaisons, the locations of the acres they farmed, the miles given over to grouse moors, the masterpieces lining their walls. Where power and privilege were not backed by generations of culture, Sabine was unyielding in her disdain. She was allergic to new money. She said it was visceral. This scorn aroused in her the nervous vigour she needed to turn away the most ostentatious parvenu.

Sabine accused our customers of being martyrs to gluttony. She said they ate with the same lack of involvement, with the same passivity, with which they absorbed conventional wisdom. 'They gather in a semblance of community, sacrificing their individuality to the power of the Establishment.' Her disrespect for the parvenu owed something to her conviction that they would be wishing to dine at Les Coteaux only because it was fashionable to do so. (I should, perhaps, mention here that Sabine hated fashion. It was style she prized.) It is true that many of our customers had no palate to speak of: they were uneducated eaters. Sabine detected in them five main ways in which they sinned by gluttony: they ate too precipitately, too expensively, too much, too eagerly and with too much fuss. She revelled in the expectation of their high blood pressure, angina and sclerosis. 'But we need them,' I protested. And she would reassure me that there would always be others to take their place. She said that if I were front-of-house, obliged to watch men and women sweating, palpitating, burping and farting in the consummation of my laboriously prepared, exquisite dishes, holding their napkins to their faces with nicotine-stained fingers, reeling from drinking too much, obese, flushed, bleary-

16

eyed, I too would be sickened. And gluttony made them irritable as well as bilious. And violent. 'They never think of anything else but of what they can consume!' she said. 'I often wonder, as our customers look furtively from one to another, if they are contemplating the taste and texture of other diners. The consoling thing about the rich and powerful is that eventually, having eaten up all the weak, they will have only themselves to consume. Then the world will be made ready for new creation. It may stand a chance.'

'What an odd country yours is!' Sabine would remark accusingly. 'Not a single millionaire is an Oxbridge graduate, and yet having made their money all they want is to appear educated. And so it is that all those who have stared uncritically from childhood at television are trustees of your major art collections and sit on the boards of your orchestras.' Did I realize, she asked me, that she could so arrange it as to have under our roof on a single evening the front bench, the Arts Council and six members of the royal family and poison the lot? Whereas these customers were the very *champignons* essential to Sabine, she nevertheless complained that their behaviour failed to reflect their oft-quoted belief in the sense of personal responsibility the rest of us were meant to display. Added to which, it set her teeth on edge to listen to their neighing upper-class accents and stuttering affectations. Why did so many affect speech deformity? Why pretend not to be able to pronounce an 'r', a 'th' or a 'v'? What was smart about that? The British were unfathomable. Was it a badge worn by the upper classes to distinguish themselves from the under-upper class? And her jaw shut fast-clenched.

Sabine could not tolerate customers whose conversation revolved around diets ('There is only one thing more difficult than keeping to a diet, which is not imposing it

17

on others.'), and she was particularly intolerant of anyone who asked for margarine for his roll. She quivered with irritation on hearing someone was teetotal. How would he digest and, therefore, properly appreciate my food without wine to accompany its passage? As for the smoker! How could he taste if he smoked? To taste, he must first smell the scents that emanate from my dishes, then savour the texture and variety of my foods that emerge to arouse the taste-buds, and carefully swallow small portions (above all small) to allow the combination of flavours to pass beneath the nasal channel. Only then should he swallow. She was right: she knew it all. But I begged her to control her urge to say all this within earshot of our customers.

When a known politician dining at Les Coteaux was accompanied by an unfamiliar face, whose credit card was presented to settle the bill, Sabine recorded that a man of the utmost importance in the Ministry of Toads had signed the authorization. She would accept reservations only from those who would not check their bills. 'Only those who do not ask the price can afford ours,' she used to say. And where she suspected a certain tightness of fist, she would quote my dearest master Antoine Carême: *'L'homme riche et avare vit dans la médiocrité et meut de même.'* In the category of the avaricious, she included those with a participle but no pence to their names, who expected special allowance to be made for them. (One of these was known to eat before entering the restaurant, so as to order less and thus pay less.) She was uncompromising. It was not that she would overcharge a customer, or charge him for an item he had not ordered or even for a dish he had not enjoyed. No, Sabine was not like that. It was her intention that everything at Les Coteaux should always be above reproach. No customer must have cause to complain. In the rare event she foresaw the merest reproach on the farthest horizon, she would arrange her face in a professional smile and convey friendly concern for an imagined oversight, and watch the reproach fade. Had she, in the most unlikely event, found herself at greater disadvantage than this, she would never have shown it.

Sabine detected the artist in me before I detected it myself. She fell in love with it. She wanted it. I was astonished, overwhelmed by her admiration. In giving myself to her, to do with whatever she chose, I felt I was dedicating myself to perfection, for Sabine has it all: beauty, intelligence, courage. She is exquisite. I was all too willing to worship at her feet. It is only now that I ask myself whether I was not a little too ready to relinquish my independence. There is nothing left within me that Sabine has not rearranged.

For example, how was it that, being so utterly English in all respects, I was sucked so easily into the slipstream of the great French masters? I cannot account for it, unless it was Sabine who, without my being aware, launched me in that direction. Whatever the case, within a few years of first encountering his work, it was as if the soul of Carême had entered my body and taken command of my culinary aptitude. Celebrity shone so splendidly and warmly on Carême, it cast a long shadow. I felt his shadow was my guardian. I never wanted one of my own. My deepest affection is still reserved for him above all others. Like me, he was the child of a poor working man, weighed down by progeny and unable to feed them all. He wrote: 'Although born into one of the poorest families of France, of a family of twenty-five children, although my father literally threw me into the street to save me, fortune smiled very soon upon me and a good fairy has often taken me by the hand to lead me to the goal.'

And so it was for me. My family, too poor to cope with the seventh of seven children, gave me to a pious aunt who had no children of her own and wanted the gift of a strong lad to be her unpaid servant. And as with Carême, fortune smiled on me in my misery. I, too, liked hard work. I did my best at school; I did my best for Aunt. Hard work distracted me from my unfortunate circumstances. Food had to be prepared and Aunt was unskilled. Living on potatoes and cabbages, I determined to turn necessity into virtue and be vegetarian for life, for was Paradise not vegetarian? In childishness, I imagined that this commitment might ameliorate my standing with God. In the event, it did not. I grew older but neither richer nor happier. I noticed, as God himself had noticed, that 'man's imagination is evil from his youth'. I reckoned that along with the evident failings which denied me the promise of Paradise eventually, and something which fell only reasonably short of it in the present, I might go unpunished were I to taste meat. And since Western man has been doing just that since Noah's day, and developed something of a hunger for it, I left behind my credulous faith.

Nor was I satisfied to continue to produce the kind of food eaten in the slums of the provinces where I was growing up. I borrowed books from the lending library and learnt how to transform the cheap ingredients Aunt could afford. By the time I was fifteen and leaving school, it was assumed by Aunt and my teachers that I would earn my living as a cook. Nor did it occur to me that other openings were available to me. Anyhow, I could not imagine anything more absorbing. Eventually, I found cooking both mentally and physically fulfilling. I dedicated myself willingly to discipleship and committed to memory the work of many dead masters. And as I re-created their masterpieces, correct in every detail, I fancied I received the satisfaction of Grantz, Lobella, Burghart and, most particularly, Carême. And you will have observed, I was discriminating from the start. Not for me the excesses of a Soyer, not for me his 'fantasies'. No boar's head modelled in sponge cake, masked with chocolate icing with pastel tusks, red-cherry eyes and pistachio eyebrows. No turkey stuffed with boneless duck stuffed with boneless pheasant, quail, snipe, woodcock and pigeon braised in green turtle fat, with truffle garnished with cockscombs, served with asparagus sauce. Such showing-off was always repulsive to me.

In the physical rather than the metaphysical application of my vocation, I enjoyed the early rising to market to select the fruit and vegetables, the meat, fish and poultry worthy of my mentors. I felt myself a man when I parried with suppliers and got my way. I would return to the kitchen in a state of excitation, eager to transform prime materials into facsimiles of celebrated inventions. My soul went into my cooking. I had taken trouble to ensure that the sucking-pig was new-born, that the flesh of the mature animals and fruit was *à point*, and my pheasants decomposing. And if my customers wanted to believe that truffles were an aphrodisiac, I did nothing to discourage Sabine contributing to the deception, or even embroidering it with the evidence that to achieve a particularly satisfying effect they should be eaten *sous la cendre*. What, I asked myself, could be more meaningful than to devote myself to re-creating the art of genius?

It therefore threw me into terrible confusion (indeed, I felt sabotaged) when Sabine said quite baldly that instead of following my masters' recipes, I should invent my own. Why? Were those of Carême not good enough for our customers? What had *les champignons* to complain about? Were we not booked solid for weeks? Were my fidelity and discrimination to be thus rewarded? What did Sabine mean by this betrayal? My head reeled, I found myself in no man's land, sensing the taste of combinations I could

21

not identify. I was being dragged to the edge of the abyss. The business of invention is woman's work. I did not work to become a woman but a man.

Sabine noted my consternation. She said it was a passing phase and I would get over it. She administered . . . I forget the name of the tablets. I made no objection. I saw no point. There is no gainsaying Sabine. Once she gets an idea into her head it is set in concrete. She always observed me too intently, as if I were a child. She interested herself in every detail regarding my health, from my teeth (rotting, owing to poor diet in early childhood) to my bowels (regular). And I preferred to avoid the unwelcome sensation that flowed from contradicting her. I would never have consulted a doctor. I had had little experience of medical men.

But I owed it to Sabine not to crack up. There was Les Coteaux to consider.

Until then all the food columnists shared the opinion that Les Coteaux was in every detail the finest restaurant in the country. Food, appointments, service, all were impeccable. The setting a delight. Since receiving our fourth star we had not suffered the hint of a reproach. It came, I imagine, as completely unforeseen to Sabine when a critic, with something of an over-fondness for alcohol and after an infamous bout of unrequited love, unburdened his spleen on us. He addressed his reader 'Dear Gastronome', alerting him in his opening sentence to our prices and expressing the view that 'no meal can ever be worth that sum'. He singled out for particular scorn 'the chef's unswerving devotion, amounting to unseemly hero-worship, to the heavy, bourgeois cooking beloved of the Victorians'.

'I noticed he ate like a horse!' Sabine said, throwing

the paper across the room. 'And *he* didn't settle the bill.'

I was surprised that Sabine had found a *couvert* for him in the first place. His reputation went before him, as did his suspicion of French culture and general dislike of 'abroad'. She explained that he had taken the precaution of accompanying a party of eight, which included the Secretary of State for Roads and Lord X, the millionaire head of a major construction company. Sabine, being particularly interested in what those two might be plotting, rather overlooked the need to flatter the newspaperman. 'Dear Gastronome', as he was henceforth dubbed, would never again succeed in getting a table at Les Coteaux, even if it meant refusing him the menu once he was seated under an assumed name and wearing the false beard he was known to adopt when pushed. 'Dear Gastronome' had seriously blotted his copy-book with my wife, who remarked of him that she had been hypnotized by his dirty finger-nails and Burton's suit and on neither count had felt inclined to pass the time of day with him. But looking back, I believe Sabine was whistling in the dark. She never once referred to his criticism, but I know she had not cared for the word 'Victorians'.

Sabine evolved a way of making suggestions tentatively, even slyly. I felt I was being seduced. She said: 'You are so gifted! You could do anything!' But I felt that while she said those things she was trying to convince herself as much as me.

I need to know precisely, a priori, what the result of my endeavour will be, how it will taste, how it will appear. I am not daring by nature. If I attested to something in 1942, I am likely to cleave to that view until I die. I despise capriciousness. Miscellaneous objects thrown together in a drawer depress me.

While conducting her *marivaudage*, Sabine never tired of reminding our customers that cooking is a language through which a society expresses itself. For fifteen years, while she beamed her charming if professional smile on a fawning diner, she made the point that 'Chef would never deviate from his adherence to the French masters'. She conveyed without further comment her view that only French cuisine (and thus French culture in general) existed. I had wondered whether our customers might not regard her insistence on this point as personally insulting. Sabine assured me it was not the case. The English were not only food snobs but masochists. Furthermore, whatever their national pride, they knew *au fond* that French culture was more sophisticated than English and imagined that by eating the food of France they absorbed with it the cave paintings of Lascaux, the châteaux of the Loire, the court of Versailles – even Christian Dior. Sabine's snobbism was as flexible as it was durable. And then, out of the blue and in marked contrast to these deeply held convictions, she was asking me to invent dishes. Me! A mere Englishman . . . in England . . . cultureless.

I cannot stand contradictions. I like order. I like certainties. My preferred reading is manifestos. I expect the successful party in an election to keep its promises. When Sabine talks of the need for change, I note the sweat in the palms of my hands, the pounding of my heart, the pain at my temples. I believe in systems. I know from experience that it is chemistry which rules the success of my cooking. I like to think of the days of Empire, of imperialism. Too much freedom, I say, is a bad thing.

After all, I had been involved in my career for fifteen years. I had brought to near-perfection my ability to produce dishes faithful to the recipes of the past, yet palatable to the taste of the present. Such dedication is a private matter, affirmed in solitude. I did not want Sabine looking over my shoulder, questioning, making suggestions. To be a disciple is to adopt an unquestioning stance. I dreaded Sabine might interpose further ideas and so one morning I withdrew where she could not find me. I had no other motive for locking myself away for four hours. But how could I confide this to her? I had no wish to hurt her. It is perhaps not surprising that, unable to account for my unusual behaviour, she put it down to derangement.

And then one day when I was trying to work out precisely how Carême would wish me to dress a particularly fine turbot, Sabine came into the kitchen with a book under her arm: *The Dishes of Fung Lo*. Now, I am ready to accept that the ancient courts of China were as gastronomically refined as those anywhere in the world, and I believe this with all my heart, but no European could ever, were he so to wish, reproduce their food authentically. It is too far removed from our culture. It may well be, indeed, that our very taste-buds have so evolved as to be unable to unfold to tastes such as theirs. And why not? We do not press our women's feet into shoes too small for them or sleep on the floor with bricks for pillows. We are hardly likely to appreciate the brains of a live monkey.

Notwithstanding, I did start to experiment. I had to, for her. My inventions did not work out. I was not used to failure and it made a wreck of me. Sabine insisted: 'You see! Mark my words. It may take a little time. Eventually, you will succeed.' Meanwhile she administered medication to calm my nerves. 'Your evident and accelerating dissatisfaction with yourself is a danger to you, my poor chef!' she reprimanded kindly. She was looking worried.

I imagined I was concealing my self-loathing. I thought I swore inwardly. I thought I wept silently. I did not know that Sabine was aware that I had collapsed on finding that my *sauce angélique* was inedible and had wept tears of humiliation.

Sauce angélique was among my first inventions. I designed it for my *filet de sole en papillote* and for my *oeufs en cocotte*. I had always obtained my saffron from a supplier in the Gatinais and for years had had no reason to complain about its quality. But the moment I *invented* a sauce, fate intervened to render it inedible. (Were my masters involved?) I examined the stock: perfect. I examined the Jersey cream: likewise perfect. I poured the spices out of their containers and examined them. Nothing wrong there. And then I inspected the saffron. The little flecks of dried stamen were redder than they should have been. Clearly, they had been adulterated. With safflower. An old trick. One of the oldest. One to make this gold dust yet more costly. There was nothing for it but to pour my sauce down the drain and strike the *filet de sole* and *oeufs* off the menu.

Sabine registered the disaster and took over. She contacted other suppliers – her first foray into this area of our business. But she never did succeed in obtaining the absolutely pure product my sauce demanded. She complained that I had over-reacted. She told me I would and should invent something else, equally imaginative but without saffron. I was not so sure. All this talk of invention was intolerable to me. I became increasingly agitated. What next would fail me, I asked myself? If I were to present my raw materials less elaborately than had my masters, every single ingredient had to be *à la perfection*. And then to my horror I noticed that my berry dealer was not getting the *fraises des bois* to me the day they were picked. The Argenteuil asparagus proved unreliable, too; while examining the tinges of ultramarine and rosy pink at their heads, I found too much dusting of sand.

26

The stalks were nicely blanched, but there was something lifeless about the bunches, none the less. As for the baby turnips for my winter goose dishes, although my supplier insisted they had been raised in the soil of Meaux, my palate refuted him. I bought only those the size of a Victoria plum, but even they were over-pungent.

My lifelong dedication to the preparation of food had made me sensitive to the beauty of fresh vegetables and herbs and to consideration for the welfare of animals bred for the table. I supported those whose mission it was to see that the rivers and oceans were kept free from pollution. I had respect for chefs who, in the face of an undemanding and indifferent clientele, persisted in doing their best. I myself kept out of the restaurant for fear that were I to come into close contact with my customers their standards might undermine my determination to maintain the highest, despite their inability to judge. Because Les Coteaux was fashionable, they were liable to heap praise on anything we served, and Sabine had impressed on me never to allow myself to be submerged by the commonplace. I took this to heart, whereas everything she reported to me about my customers I allowed myself to register only on the surface. And I let Sabine do my resenting for me.

I stopped buying at Covent Garden and relied on French suppliers who flew their produce direct to me. And two English market gardeners in East Anglia who delivered. The Englishmen, however, seemed incapable (Sabine said unwilling) of taking seriously my protestation that for an establishment such as Les Coteaux only prime produce would do. I told them that if I could not rely on waxy potatoes (I prefer the *jaune longue de Holland*, but these days it is useless to specify a variety and I was willing to make do with another if it was indistinguishable from my preference) or on a sweet, small pea (*pois*

Michaux would have been ideal), I would have to close down and then where would we all be?

I cannot pretend to have made much of an impression on either Mr Jenkins or Mr Bowles. Neither understood that it is not worth my going to the trouble I take if in the first place the ingredients I am supplied with are second rate. 'Who's going to notice?' asked Mr Bowles. 'You don't imagine your customers are that fastidious, do you?' And he went on to count off on his fingers the other restaurateurs he supplied to their complete satisfaction. 'No one else has ever complained.'

When I repeated this conversation to Sabine, she advised me not to enter into further discussion with these men. 'Throw out what's not up to standard!' She said that she would add what we lost to the cost of my dishes. Sabine would never descend to arguing with a supplier or a customer. In fact, as I mentioned, she had little if any contact with suppliers. She did, however, buy our wine, direct from châteaux in France, Germany and Switzerland. We had an exceptionally fine cellar, thanks to my wife.

I am ready to admit that Sabine probably knew me better than I knew myself. But following the disaster with my *sauce angélique* and my foolish outbursts, I thought her claim that I was 'harbouring thoughts of eternal rest' way over the top. It is true, I had become agitated and depressed. No doubt my anxiety made her anxious but, oddly, this did nothing to discourage Sabine from positively reactivating it. She insisted I create *la nouvelle cuisine Coteaux*. I never said as much but I was pretty sure that her obstinacy owed itself as much to 'Dear Gastronome' as to her desire for me to reveal my capacity for creativity. And while she nagged me to invent rather than interpret, she may have been trying to justify to herself that I was worth her trouble. After each assault, she would leave the room quickly, not wanting to become involved in contention. I wonder now whether she was beginning to realize that were I the artist she wanted to make of me, I would never have succumbed to her, never allowed her to reinvent me. I would have bothered her with my initiative.

If I am not mistaken, it was one Sunday afternoon that Sabine suggested a walk in the park. We sat overlooking the Round Pond and she confided to me her belief that I needed psychological treatment, distractions and a rest. In that order. Well, whereas I acquiesced quite graciously in taking the tablets she gave me at night, I was not going to put myself in the hands of someone who would try to control my mind. Nor would I waste my time on classes in fretwork, meditation and/or genealogy. I could not see how we could possibly close the restaurant for a month. Sabine argued that were I not to divert myself from my anxious thoughts, I might 'do something foolish'. In this I judged her somewhat hysterical, although I did not say so. I had no anxieties, that is if only she would put a stop to her efforts to get me to renounce my affiliation to my masters. I was not going to be brainwashed into apostasy. I dug my feet in. My obligation to my masters, to achieve the greatest verisimilitude possible in the kitchen, was absolute.

Sabine had always been a great reader. From the age of five she had had the run of her father's library, one of the greatest European libraries of gastronomy. While I lay awake at night, unable to drive the word 'invent' out of my mind, Sabine read. (She is an expert on Beauvilliers, Meot, Hennerve and Baleine.) When she was not at work, organizing the staff, attending to linen, silver, crystal and flowers, seeing to the printing of our menus and to her excessively expensive wardrobe, checking the wine in the cellar, Sabine read. When I first met her she was poring over a book; she was absorbing the example of Beauvilliers at the time. It was he who had inspired her to create Les Coteaux years before we met. And now that she was convinced I was on the verge of suicide, it was not surprising that she turned to books for information about my condition and, perhaps, for consolation. In the event it was Madame de Sévigné's account of the death of François Vatel, steward to the Prince de Condé, that held sway.

To be perfectly honest, I did identify somewhat with Vatel. I loved him first for his modesty. For all his accomplishments, too. After all, *The Art of Carving* remains, after three hundred years, one of the Bibles of my profession. Vatel never forgot that he was self-taught. His problem, like my own, was under-confidence. He could not withstand the very idea of failure.

The King arrived on Thursday evening; the hunt, the lanterns, the moonlight, the drive, the meal in a place carpeted with jonquils – it was all one could wish for. They had supper: at some tables there was no roast, because several unexpected guests had turned up. Vatel was greatly disturbed; he said several times: 'My honour is ruined; this is a disgrace I cannot endure. My head is spinning. I have not slept for twelve nights.'

Despite reassurances, Vatel was mortified. He went up to his room, put his sword against the door and thrust it through his heart. Three times.

30

It was extraordinary that someone like me should have met someone like Sabine, let alone have married her. I was working as a commis chef at the Hôtel Palais, Lausanne. My chef was a decent man, who looked after his staff like a father. Noticing that I was at a loose end on my days off, he asked me one Sunday if I would care to accompany him on a hike across the hills. He was going over to the Château d'Alouettes to return a book. He was not intending to take me into the château. He had not informed Dr Widmer that he would be with an employee. Since it was a fine day I would not suffer if he left me sitting on the entrance steps for a while. 'There is a magnificent view to enjoy over the lake to the mountains beyond.' Being cooped up as I was in the kitchens all week, the idea appealed to me.

I could not have been enjoying the view for more than ten minutes before Dr Widmer spotted me from the library window and asked Bouloux who I was and what I was doing there. On being told, he beckoned me to the front entrance. I was not used to the kindness of strangers. I was embarrassed. I had nothing to say to my host. But kind Dr Widmer overlooked this and led me into the library.

Dr Widmer was in his fifties. He was a fine-looking man with a neat beard. He wore a noticeably well-cut suit and moved enveloped in an invisible cloud of sandalwood. I had the feeling he had never so much as brushed against need, let alone poverty. He had come from a learned background. Books meant more to him than people. 'You must learn the history of your craft!' he advised, and started forthwith on my education.

Dr Widmer's oak-panelled library of cookery books, manuscripts and herbals was world famous. He had first editions of Taillevent, Escoffier, Carême (who was to become my dearest master) and Couffe, not to mention

31

The Forme of Cury, the fourteenth-century English masterpiece. He had recently acquired Grimod de la Reynière's work. He had had to wait for a fine copy, not wishing for a more easily obtainable worn one, he explained. He showed me *Le ménagier de Paris* (1393) and Rosselli's *Epulario*. He was clearly intoxicated by these acquisitions. I recall the oddly passionate manner in which he opened up for me *Küchenmeisterei*, an anonymous publication in five parts, dated 1484. He encouraged me to dip into these volumes with him, to enjoy as he enjoyed, not only the information they supplied but the paper on which they were written, the quality of the ink, the little illustrations, the colour of the binding string that had come loose here and there over the years. And then, suddenly, he moved to another book-rest, another table, dragging me with him by the arm, to take me through a copy of Marx von Rupolt's *Ein neu Kochbuch* (1531) and others of his treasures whose titles now escape me. I do remember, however, the little book about the distillation of alcohol. Did I know, he asked, that it had been the Arabs who invented the process? An irony, since the majority today do not touch the stuff. It was an exquisite volume filled with diagrams of early distillation techniques.

I had to tell Dr Widmer that I had not learnt chemistry at school. I was ashamed to have to admit the fact. He understood my embarrassment and quickly passed on to a subject of his own embarrassment: his Swiss collection was unrepresentative. He had recently missed a German manuscript from the Lavater collection, and had failed to acquire something he dearly wanted from Selzer von Wintertur's library. The competition was too keen for him, the premium on Swiss material ridiculously inflated. 'I can no longer bid with the abandon I once did. The richest collectors are Swiss,' he told me. 'Xenophobes! They prize Swiss material above all other. I am going to have to be satisfied with material from the East.' And then, just before showing Bouloux and me out, he took a copy of the *Libre de Coch* (1756) from his Spanish shelf and took me through recipes for frogs, which cheered him up.

It was quite by chance that I met Dr Widmer's daughter Sabine that afternoon. She happened to be seated in a corner of the library, a book with plans of early Paris restaurants unfolded before her. She was making tracings, adapting colours and taking notes on appurtenances. She had been in the library all afternoon, but being so absorbed in her study, she had not moved and I had not noticed her.

That day turned out to be momentous. Not only did Dr Widmer launch me on my lifelong passion for the literature of my calling, from Apicius to the present, but Sabine entered my life.

I lay awake unable to erase the word 'invent' from my mind. 'Invent': a demon of a word, barbed and insistent. I attempted to overlay it with an image of a table groaning under the weight of Carême's work for the King of England, the Emperor Alexander, the whole Austrian court. What a prodigy he was! His taste for the best, the most expensive, the most elegant. Yet he had been practical and methodical. The pages of *L'art de la cuisine française* testify to that. He knew what to buy and how to buy; what to store and how to store. It was his intention that, having founded *la grande cuisine*, it should be re-created down the centuries. Today the honour and pleasure were mine! That was all I required for my peace and tranquillity. 'You only rely on Carême's inheritance,' Sabine said, 'because you have none from your family.' I failed to see the connection at the time. I could not understand her logic. 'If you stick to your beloved Carême another year, you will be stuck with him for the rest of your life!' she added. I had heard her speak like this when judging a couple's marriage: 'Once they are over the seven-year itch, they never separate!'

Was Sabine jealous of my devotion to my master? Did she want for herself the control he had for so long exercised over me? Did the concern she expressed for my sanity imply a *desire* for my suicide? If she could not get absolute control over me alive, would she prefer me dead? This uncharitable thought worried me. I did not like myself better for entertaining it. And it generated further thoughts of an unwelcome nature: once dead, Sabine would report me as she had experienced me, or as she wished others to think she had. I would exist only in her. She would find satisfaction in that. Indeed, I would have to start avoiding her embrace, for in the unlikely event that I managed to lose myself, I would be doing so to her. When she brought me my pills in the half-light of a dimmed lamp, I could see how easy it would be for her to extinguish me, easy as switching off a light. (And if Sabine forgot me, ceased to speak about me, I should cease to be spoken for.)

She was, however, right: I did have very little in the way of distractions. I was not like other men. I played no sport. I had no nights-out-with-the-boys, no pub-crawling. I had no desire for a yacht, a country house, a portfolio of shares (I had always rated 'investments' with quantity surveying as being the most boring subject in the world). I had no mistress. I did not dare. Perhaps I was too one-dimensional? I had always been satisfied with very little.

Did I overwork? We opened for dinner six nights a week. The reason we did not open at midday was that Sabine said my food was too sublime to be accompanied by talk of business and politics. Dalliance, she said, was a more fitting accompaniment. Dalliance demands time and dinner provides more than luncheon. She believed in the intimate alliance between the art of well-tuned words and the art of dining well. I had, in addition, reluctantly agreed to provide wedding breakfasts for minor royalty and although it had been, as Sabine pointed out, worthwhile for the publicity as well as the money, it meant closing the restaurant for the day and this I resented. I took my work seriously. It is not serious to produce the sort of showy wedding fare I was obliged to supply. And it was to lead to another of Sabine's ideas of which I did not entirely approve.

Sabine received a telephone call from the secretary of the Flaubert Society, a friend of the Minister for the Arts, who had been a guest at one of our most lavish wedding breakfasts. Would we be interested in re-creating the Bovary wedding feast for the event? I could hardly refuse. If I did so, I would be putting Sabine in an embarrassing position. Our instructions from the Society were to stick rigidly both to the menu and the excessive quantities involved in the original, despite the fact that even the Secretary himself doubted the forty-three members would do justice to the spread as completely as had the forty-three wedding guests at Les Bertaux. 'They are not going to take us over for sixteen hours,' Sabine reassured me. 'Nor do they wish us to transform the restaurant into a cart-shed.' She was trying to humour me.

I prepared four sirloins, six dishes of hashed chicken, some stewed veal, three legs of mutton and a roast sucking-pig flanked by four pork sausages with sorrel. I interpreted the hashed veal in a rustic Norman fashion, making liberal use of Calvados and apples. So far as the tarts and custards were concerned, I was reminded of my early life with Aunt. If only I had been able to afford then the soft Normandy cheeses and thick cream with *mirabelles* and *reine-claudes*. (There was no written evidence for these fruits and cheeses but the Secretary agreed they were most likely to have been in Flaubert's mind.)

It was the wedding-cake, a vulgar confection from Yvetot, that took my time.

It started off at the base with a square of blue cardboard representing a temple with porticoes and colonnades, with stucco statuettes all round it in recesses studded with gilt-paper stars; on the second layer was a castle keep in Savoy cakes, surrounded by tiny fortifications in angelica, almonds, raisins and quarters of orange; and finally, on the uppermost platform, which was a green meadow with rocks, pools of jam and boats of nutshell, stood a little Cupid, poised on a chocolate swing whose uprights had two real rose-buds for knobs at the top.

During the first flush of Sabine's enthusiasm for her literary luncheons, I well remember the Jane Austen occasion, for I particularly resented having to prepare that meal. I was asked for ox-cheek and dumplings and baked *everything*: apples, custard, biscuits. And a sweetbread fricassee and a boiled (*sic*) fowl with oyster sauce. The rest escapes me, as well it might. So disturbed by these concoctions, I was curious to see the members of the Jane Austen Society tucking in. They appeared as inelegant as the food they specified. The young women were without make-up, in pleated skirts, twin-sets and sensible shoes. They were accompanied by rather older men with loud, piping voices, dressed in heavy tweeds, some with garish waistcoats, all with watch-chains.

I felt more in harmony with Nana's dinner for the Zola Society. Zola had taken the precaution to include the menu of an actual meal in his novel, one prepared at Brébant's, a popular restaurant with the Bohemian society of Paris in the 1880s. The menu was well balanced and conveyed well-being. Other groups, societies and dining-clubs attached to other authors involved me in the less rewarding tasks I had undertaken for the Jane Austen Society. I am reminded, particularly, of the Trollope Diners, the Walter Scott Table (Bag-pudding, Loch Fyne herrings and boiled sheep's head), the Virginia Woolf Association and the Pope and Thackeray Clubs. Then there was the Roman dinner, dedicated to Hera, taken from the *Chansons de geste*, involving roasted peacock with pepper sauce and gilded egg yolks. . . .

The preparation of the medieval feasts gave me little satisfaction. The taste of the dishes was repulsive to my palate. Dates do *not* enhance salmon and eels, figs are *not* improved by being prepared with pepper and ginger, and I do not like fruit pies to be seasoned with herbs. And far too much emphasis is placed on the appearance of food in this period of history. I did as I was asked, none the less. I refeathered the fowl to make them appear alive, but with their claws and beaks gleaming with gold (it was only paper). I served the birds on huge pewter platters with golden apples (meat balls wrapped in more of the same paper) with tinted green pastry leaves. I had spit-roasted the suckling-deer whole. Lying on its bed of watercress, it reminded me of a domestic cat luxuriating in the sun. I felt quite sick. Four bearers carried my pastry unicorn into the dining-room on a rushed board. I had set the animal in a garden with fruit trees against pastry walls, with herbs in a chequer-board pattern growing from raised pastry beds. Loud applause greeted each of my confections as they were borne in aloft.

To welcome the company, the Medieval Society had one of their members dressed as a surveyor. He placed the salt in position and ushered the more senior members

37

of the Society to be seated above it. I watched as he waved his key to summon the pantler, who was in charge of the bread. This individual was dressed with a long fringed fabric over his shoulder in which he carried the loaves. He cut the upper crust from my spiced loaves and presented them to the seniors and then made trenchers for the others. These trenchers would have found their way to the poor, but it was the scholars who fell upon them that afternoon.

They had a laverer and aquamande with bowls of fragrant water for the washing of hands. An important discussion ensued as to which fingers were to be used for which dishes. The carver came forward to break the deer in pieces, wing the partridges and unbrace the mallard. The knives he wore on his belt jingled like those on the belt of a goaler. Then came the cup-bearer to test the wine. Consternation! They were lacking a clergyman. A stupid oversight! It would have been so easy to have found one. The music that should have been supplied by costly musicians was also lacking, but at least Sabine had had the foresight to provide a gramophone.

There is nothing at which some scholars will not stop. I was asked to produce an Islamic feast based on twelfth-century poetry, in which the poet excites his beloved with saffron rice and pieces of meat impaled on a skewer crowned with a lump of fatty sheep's tail, intestine, onions and chick peas and, to round off, pickled fruits. I avoided entering the dining-room that day. I heard it had been turned into a highly scented place with divans and cushions. I could imagine the rest.

It was as a result of this exotic feast and the publicity it attracted (its authenticity was particularly appreciated) that Sabine was approached by anthropologists, lawyers and doctors to create occasions peculiar to their professions. One man came in person to request a re-enactment of a celebration that had taken place at Maxim's in Paris. *The maître d'hôtel* had served a naked girl covered in cherry sauce to a millionaire. 'A rich dish that cried, Come, eat me!' I put my foot down. I foresaw problems. There are freakish people about. I had heard that human flesh was being consumed in London. It was not generally known and it was a rare occurrence but it was going on among occultists. I dreaded being approached with unidentifiable meat and being asked to prepare it. I was well aware that in the far-flung places of the world it was quite the thing to eat the brains of the dead, to fortify oneself against their revenge, and I knew the Ancient Greeks served up their illegitimate children and unfaithful wives and mistresses in pies, stews and on spits. I forbade Sabine to take reservations from the Atreus Society. My knowledge of cannibalism led me to wonder how in the so-called civilized world these impulses are gratified. But I did not want a practical demonstration. I was not going to agree to so much as a mock-up for an anthropological society.

The precariousness of my position was brought to my attention forcefully one day when a man arrived at the tradesmen's entrance to Les Coteaux and hoodwinked a member of my team into fetching me to the door. Dr Boyle was a member of a Zoological Society. He carried with him a jug of elephant's milk. Would I be so good as to make him a type of Russian cream for which he had a recipe in his pocket? He would pay me well. Fortunately, I had my wits about me and sent him packing. I learnt subsequently that this man had quite a reputation as a public nuisance. He was in the habit of accosting nursing mothers on park benches for their milk. On being reported to the police and warned that his behaviour would lead to his prosecution, he arranged with one of the keepers at the zoo to be kept supplied with elephants' milk, the sweetest next to human kind. Tired of drinking it neat, as it were, he hankered for it to be turned into exotic dishes and sought out celebrated cooks to do this for him.

I learnt of another of Dr Boyle's clan. A man who skinned his feet, fried the parings and added them as croutons to his salads. And another who took blood from his veins to seethe his steaks and use as a basis for sauces. I cannot bring myself to repeat all that was related to me. I did not confide it to Sabine. I was disturbed by the information and when I did snatch sleep it was accompanied by nightmares.

Had I given in to Sabine and employed the whole *brigade de cuisine* a restaurant seating eighty demands, I might have survived. But I felt the need to have absolute control over everything in the kitchen. I was not only the *gros bonnet* but the sauce chef, *entremetteur*, *rôtisseur* and *garde-manger*. It was too great a load to shoulder, even though I had a commis attached to each *partie*, and excellent maids-of-all-work to do the donkey-work. Beyond the green baize door, Sabine, who characterized her role at Les Coteaux as a 'nightly performance in light comedy' (one for which her unswerving self-confidence served her particularly well, I thought), moved resolutely between the tables and chairs like a side-winder rattlesnake.

Sabine had an unquenchable thirst for the limelight, to be seen but not touched. To this end she cultivated a stylish simplicity that few women can achieve, even when they identify it as desirable. Five foot eight, long necked with a head like that of Nefertiti, Sabine was dressed by Worth and Patou. Her hands looked as if they had never done a day's work. Her complexion appeared to be without make-up, so skilfully did she apply the costly Swiss products she preferred. She would welcome every customer personally. She would seem to discuss with him which table he would like to occupy. In fact, she invariably

40

managed to lead him to the table she had already reserved for him and his party. Once dinner was progress-
ing satisfactorily, and her roles as hostess, trouble-shooter
and expert on food and wine were no longer called for,
she repaired to the glassed-in cubicle, something on the
lines of a sedan chair, that she had designed for an al-
cove in the dining-room, from which she had an uninterrupted view of diners and staff alike. There she made
out the bills.

It has been accurately noted, I think, that anyone can
learn to cook but a good restaurateur is born. I learnt
my *métier* laboriously, over many years, under a succession of chefs. Sabine was born to her vocation. From the
moment she read about the restaurant Beauvilliers opened
in Paris in 1784, she determined to become a restaurateur in his mode: to run the very best establishment somewhere in the world. Some might wonder why it was that
Sabine married me and opened a restaurant for me. (I
think I am wise to say 'for' rather than 'with' me, because I would have been happy enough to carry on as a
commis in the kitchens of any good restaurateur.) It was
Sabine who insisted it was preposterous for me to go
through life as an employee. 'You deserve to derive the
full rewards of your talent!' Quoting Francesco Leonardi,
she said: 'In this world it is not your nationality that
makes you what you are but your talent', adding that I
could not be held responsible for the inconvenient fact
that I had been born in England. But I think it was she
who needed Les Coteaux. She had detected my culinary
skill before she had tasted my food. Since when, much
as she enjoyed my food, I believe she salivated more
copiously at the thought of the celebrity it attracted and
the money it made than over the contemplation of my
dishes. She must have felt quite desperate, watching me
crumble.

41

She asked me to move into the spare room. Nights, she said, had become intolerable. I sang out, I roared instructions to my staff, and was generally what she termed 'over-extended'. As I mentioned earlier, she wanted me to get away for a while. 'You speak to yourself a good deal more than you speak to me!' she complained.

Did she know that my headaches were getting worse? Had she noticed my digestion was failing? I cannot imagine she had seen that my right hand had developed a tremor so marked as to agitate my little saucepan over the heat without my having to shake it, for she rarely entered the kitchen. I saw myself like one of those ancient Chinese celadine bowls covered in hair cracks: a cracked greenhorn.

I had felt exiled long before I was. For years I had seen myself as part of a world-wide community of chefs, from Roman times and *De Re Culinaria* to Carême and *Le pâtissier pittoresque*. On one occasion I had even allowed myself to be bullied into judging a food trial: the Golden Black Pudding Contest. Sabine insisted that my four stars brought with them certain obligations and I had to represent Britain in the food stakes and Britain was trying to sell black pudding to France, rather an unfair exchange for *foie gras*, Pont-l'Evêque and vintage wines. In the event, I had to swallow sixty pieces of black pudding over two days and was ill for twenty-eight. The assault on my tastebuds was so damaging, for days I could not check the seasoning of my own cooking.

It was not only my fear of being identified that kept me out of the dining-room when my customers were at table. I was frightened of being overcome by women's scent. Scent has the effect of throwing me into a rage. I have always been frightened I might forget myself and strike the offender. Sabine never wears scent. She says the aroma of food and wine should never be polluted, even by cigars, although she is obliged to tolerate them. Added to which I feel comfortable only in my overalls. I doubt that the sort of customers we attracted would have had much respect for a man in stained white overalls.

I sometimes look back and wonder if I did not choose my *métier* for the overalls it allowed me to wear continuously. When I was eight, I spent some time in hospital. I had an operation on my throat. Everyone around me, orderlies, nurses and doctors, wore white from head to foot, and fed me on white ice-cream. Sore throat notwithstanding, it was a dazzling experience, quite the most pleasurable of my childhood. I was the centre of attraction for numberless adults. I think this may have had something to do with my choice of *métier*: food, attention, dazzling white. . . .

I never wished to overhear my customers' conversations. Sabine warned me: 'They drip like taps!' And repeated their litanies. Nor did I wish to conduct postmortems with Sabine on their preoccupations. I was not equal to her analyses. Sabine is like a surgeon with a single specialty. She knows the signs, she diagnoses, she is confident which instruments to command for the dissection she will undertake. She opens up her victim with gambits sharp as scalpels and displays the offending organ, turning it this way and that, in phrases tight as forceps. Like a suction pump, she breathes in her contempt before swabbing the blood in a more conciliatory tone and stitching up the incident ready to pass on to the next victim. I am not up to this. There were occasions when a customer, observing Sabine's authority, would attempt to take her to one side and seek her advice on a personal matter. This appalled her. She could not abide the sort of person who reveals his inner life: 'One needs an outer life for daily purposes,' she protested to me.

And while Sabine reported such matters, my attention

43

wandered and I would stare out into the street. I could not fail to be impressed by its well-ordered cleanliness. Everything in its place: a post-box at one corner, a fire hydrant at the other. I considered our customers and their enthusiasm for my food. The success we were enjoying . . . the stability. Yet while I consoled myself, I did so against a background of fear. I sensed latent violence. It starts with a sort of juvenile boisterousness, of the sort one associates with the better public schools, and deteriorates into the bullying one associates with the minor public schools and state schools. It matures at Oxford and Cambridge where the undergraduates drink until leg-over time, when they leap into the cars they have not had to pay for and drive to bed-sit land and the nurses they will not marry. Where does this lead? To Westminster. To the merchant banks. To the helm of industry. There will be no aimlessness. No sense of the pulse. Only purpose. I know about purpose but do not recognize my own in theirs. If only she would stop talking *at* me, would brew her coffee and bake her brioches and spoon the quince preserve I made last summer on to a little Copenhagen dish, but I will not, cannot resolutely refuse to discuss the Minister of Art's impending divorce. 'Dot says we are in for some scorching days. Says she can feel it in her shoulder.' Dot, one of our washers-up, is almost uncanny in her sensitivity to all but linen tea-towels and our china and glass. None the less, I turn on the ventilator over the back door. I am a martyr to women.

And then it was I started to dread rising. I carried with me a feeling that I was doomed. I focused all my attention on my *métier* but found myself in a state of near-paralysis. I veered from being highly lucid to being highly confused. Things either appeared grey and menacing or absurdly bright. On some days I felt overwhelmed by attachments, on others that I was alone in the world. I

44

was grateful that my repertory of dishes was larger and more mature than that of my feelings.

Sabine pats me on the shoulder. She is murmuring something I do not hear but whose tones are affectionate and concerned. And now I do hear every word: she is telling me that we are going to close the restaurant for a month. She will go and stay at the Château d'Alouettes, which her father left to the Swiss nation as a centre for gastronomic studies. I will go to the Hollenhof, at Hoffenberg, for a rest. 'You are making yourself ill with your obsession,' she tells me. She does not understand that I get tired of everything that does not come to completion in myself, that I have to go to the ultimate limit in my work. 'If a painter or a writer works at his craft sixteen hours a day, or an instrumentalist practises all day, he is regarded as dedicated.' I object. (I would never venture to put a foot forward if not for my work.) 'Why if a chef works sixteen hours a day in his kitchen, perfecting the recipes of the past, does his wife label him obsessional, close his restaurant and organize a holiday he does not wish to take?' (Carême's *sauce à l'espagnole* took him four days to prepare.) In my heart I believed that the mere drawing up of her plans would suffice for my change. How wrong I was!

Take away my Carême, take away my confidence.

PART TWO

Much Madness is divinest Sense –
To a discerning Eye –
Much Sense – the starkest Madness –
'Tis the Majority
In this, as All, prevail –
Assent – and you are sane –
Demur – you're straightway dangerous –
And handled with a Chain –

Emily Dickinson

Sabine does not fly. She feels out of control in the air. And so we travelled to Lausanne by boat and train. I slept soundly. The tablets Sabine gave me were effective and the rhythm of the train consoling. When I was a child at Aunt's, my little bedroom window opened on to railway lines. Every night I urged myself to sleep on board the trains that swept past ten or fifteen minutes after I got into bed, dreaming that I would fetch up somewhere far away, somewhere green and warm. All through the night, half asleep and half awake, I chimed to the *dedumdedumdedum* of wheels on track, excited by the whistle as the train entered the tunnel and my nostrils filled with sulphurous fumes. I had not taken a holiday for longer than I could remember. I had not chosen to take one now. I did not want to think about the next four weeks and sought comfort in thinking back. For all that childhood was pinched, I was less frightened then.

I must have been fast asleep, for Sabine had to shake me to rouse me. Throughout breakfast in the dining-car I felt drowsy. I would have given a lot to go back to sleep and the day before the word 'invent' invaded my life.

It was 14th May. The date showed on the town hall clock. Sabine accompanied me to the coach station. It was she who located the Hoffenberg coach in its bay. Passengers were already embarking. I put down my suitcase where they had left theirs, by the door to the hold. Sabine took my arm and drew me to her and pecked my cheek. I was surprised by her gesture. She did not normally approve of public display. But I noticed we were standing in the midst of a crowd of men, women and children running hither and thither noisily, anxiously seeking out their coaches and not taking the least notice of anyone else. 'I shall take a taxi,' Sabine said, unnecessarily. Of course she would. There was no other way of getting to the Château d'Alouettes without a car.

I banged furiously on the coach window but Sabine did not hear me. She was engrossed, talking to a stranger. It was most frustrating. I banged repeatedly on the window. Indeed, I bruised the side of my hand so doing. I called her name. I kept getting up from the seat to attract her attention, up and down, up and down. It was only when the coach started to move away that Sabine looked towards me and waved. I pointed to the driver's seat. I stabbed my finger repeatedly in its direction. I mouthed slowly and clearly 'There's no driver!' But Sabine only smiled and blew me a kiss.

Of course, how silly of me, a driverless coach is no more surprising than a driverless train, and many of those are in service all over the Continent. The Europeans are so much more advanced than we. Nothing is beyond their capabilities. I settled back in my seat. The wheels of the coach rolled silently over the macadam, as if over velvet. I had never felt more drowsy.

It was dark outside when I took from the pocket at the rear of the seat in front of my own, a brochure entitled 'Holidays in Hoffenberg'. 'Hoffenberg is Switzerland's best kept secret,' it read. 'Situated above the tree-line, it is the habitat of rare medicinal and culinary plants' (Sabine always knows her stuff) 'and the lesser spotted Scargeon. It provides the perfect restorative for those forced to spend

50

the larger part of their lives living and working in an overcrowded and polluted environment.'

Evidently there was just one inn in the village: the Hollenhof. And no other for miles. With only one place in which to lodge, the village was free from the ravages of tourism. That was a comfort. On the other hand, might the problem be that in so small and remote a location I would be thrown together with others more closely than I would find tolerable? Would they organize charades in the evenings? And Scrabble? Would they be earnest primary-school teachers, engineers, psychiatric social workers and wildlife enthusiasts? Esperantists, perhaps? I felt desolate. I had been at pains to arrange my day-to-day life so as to have the very minimum of contact with others.

An official of some sort, a man in uniform (in other circumstances I would have assumed the coach-driver), had risen from his seat at the front and alighted from the coach. He was opening the hold and throwing suitcases on to the ground. I felt affronted by what appeared to me to be rather violent gestures on his part. I was the last off the coach; by the time I got to the hold my own case lay alone, unidentified. I did not follow the other passengers into the inn at once. I stood under the porch and watched the coach move off. It took the opposite direction from where it had come. It glided soundlessly behind the inn, leaving no tyre marks in the snow.

I went over the journey in my mind. For the duration of the long ascent, our coach had not passed a single vehicle coming from the opposite direction. Could it be that the road *from* Hoffenberg was a one-way pass and the road *to* Hoffenberg another? These were puzzling matters I would like to have had clarified. The surface of the road was unbroken, the coach was soundless, there was no driver. Where had I heard that it was on automatic pilot? But I was drowsy and confused. I had probably slept most of the way.

I take my place at the end of the queue. I am aware that there is some jostling towards the front. I shall keep well away from that. In any event, I believe in awaiting my turn. The guests appear rather similar, as if they were related. The men carry their passports in their right hands and their cases in their left hands. Now they are shuffling towards the reception desk. I am reminded of how, as children, we formed up like this in imitation of a steam train. Someone is very angry. He is directing blows with the palm of his hand on a brass bell. He is having no success, though; the bell does not sound. Oh my God, where is my passport? I put down my suitcase where I can feel it with my foot. I delve into my inside jacket pocket, then with both hands into the lower jacket pockets, but all I find there is a roll of mints, a handkerchief, a chemist's bill and some string. How I hate the mess! The others are signing in and relinquishing their cases to young men in grey uniforms with huge keys in white-gloved hands. I do not appear to be getting any nearer the desk myself.

The desk is extraordinarily ugly. Behind is a wall of ochrish paper files, dry as dead leaves, headed PERSONS. I wonder whether anyone ever takes down a file? If they did remove just one for examination, I believe it would crumble in the hand and all the others would fall to the ground and turn to dust.

By the time I get to the desk there is no one behind it and no one in front of it. So unpeopled is the place, suddenly it is as if it had never known the footfalls or the voices of humankind. I find myself climbing the stairs to the fourth floor, resting on each landing on account of the weight of my suitcase. What has Sabine packed?

All the doors along the north corridor are closed. I turn east and then south and eventually in the west corridor I see a door ajar. I push it open. I am in my room. I call it 'my' room because I put down my case there. However, my problems are by no means over. What am I to do, now that I have a room? What is expected of me? Should I leave my case here, in the middle of the floor, abandon it, withdraw, return to the foyer? I cannot; I have no key with which to lock my case. I had best sit down on the bed. But for how long? I place my hands on my knees and examine the skin on the backs, skin that seems too generous for the size of my hands. I look up, to the back of the door, hoping to find instructions: notification of the times of meals, what number to ring for room service, the price of laundering a shirt. That kind of thing. But there is nothing, no instructions of any kind, not even what to do in case of fire. No telephone. No bell. Not that I would wish to summon anyone to my room. (I can't bear that even when Sabine and I are together. I don't like waiters to see her in her nightdress.)

Suddenly I notice in the corner of the room on the wall about five feet from the floor a sort of wheel with a handle attached. I rise to examine it. There is a label stuck to the handle: FOR USE IN EMERGENCIES ONLY. What does that imply? My God! Emergencies. But would I recognize one of these? I am at the window. I stare down on to the well of brick walls. On each of the three sides I see that the windows are shut and the curtains drawn. I draw my curtains. Through a slit I peer to see whether anyone across the well is observing me. I feel a sort of terror: I must get out.

I put my hand on the door handle and turn. It does not engage the lock but swings round in the palm of my hand. I am a prisoner. Am I going to be prisoner here for ever? I feel my chest tighten. I am sweating. My mouth is dry. There is no corner of this room upon which I can bear to let my glance settle and there is no view outside the window.

Just as I am absorbed, meditating on the hopelessness of my situation, I become conscious of the wardrobe literally swelling with pride. Soon it will occupy the entire space of the room. I shall be squashed flat against the wall. I do not want to acknowledge its polished obesity, or imagine how I would feel flattened against its wood belly and brass handles. I turn away, but not in time to avoid seeing something flicker in its looking-glass. I pretend to ignore this. I tell myself I must not seem to be threatened, that might deter 'it' from making its whole presence visible. It is bad enough being in solitary confinement without being continuously observed.

If I had had a father and a mother. . . . If I had had a father and a mother, I would get back to them now, never to be separated again. Then I would be safe. There would be all sorts of nourishment with them. And I would sleep, long draughts of uninterrupted repose. There would be no need to struggle to understand, no need to achieve. I would just stay put with them, living their life with them, luxuriating in feelings of security.

I do not remember each individual battle I fought with the door handle to get it to engage the lock, but I must have won the war before being consumed by the wardrobe because I do remember wandering disconsolately down the corridor, nursing my blistered palm, keeping my eyes lowered so as not to attract attention, yet stepping out as if I were going somewhere purposefully. I did not want to be detected as a shadow, shuffling with no end in view, like some destitute person.

I must find a prospect more promising than the one from my room. At the top of each flight of stairs I stop

54

to peer out of the tall, thin windows that rise from floor to ceiling. The view from the barred window-panes is the same: a grey-white waste land, an ocean of turbid snow and glassy ice. Solid mist. Holding tight to the banisters to steady myself, I stop on each landing in the fervent hope that the view will have changed.

All the while I am being careful to maintain the quiet determination I am putting into my steps. Were anyone to spot me they would not register my consternation or my plans, they would assume I was on a legitimate errand. But my determination is suffering something of a set-back. I am being assailed by a tortured scream. I cannot locate its source. And doors are slamming. I feel myself convert from suppleness, as if turning from water to ice. I am grateful to the white line that runs along the floor. I shall follow it, I shall place one foot precisely in front of the other, avoiding the gutters either side where the undesirables must walk. And now I must be careful to keep some distance between myself and the group of thick-bodied women in overalls, pushing trolleys on rubber wheels, heads down, along the line.

Alone now where it is dark and deserted, where one can descend no farther, a peculiar silence prevails. I can smell putrescence. I have a torch in my hand. (Incomprehension is a dark condition.) I am more than grateful for the merest light. I can make out four windowless walls crumbling like old, hard cheese. This place is deep, airless, and its smell acrid. It makes me gasp. I can hardly breathe. I am peering into the ante-chamber to Hades. I cannot risk putting my foot down in the slippery slime. This is not a room; it is a cave hewn from the rock of the mountain. An ossuary.

I shine my torch into the corner. It lights a pile some three feet in diameter. I can make out not only kitchen detritus but bones, hundreds of bones. From what animals,

I wonder? And for what purpose are the syringes, the scalpels, the little glass phials? The blood-soaked bandages and lint make me heave. I pick my way gingerly towards an upturned packing-case. The wood planks of the case are rotting. If I stand on the thing it will almost certainly give way. Careful not to slip into the slime underfoot, avoiding the shattered glass and unsavoury ordure, I climb on to a tin drum and raise myself upright. The ceiling is low. I must mind my head.

I shine the torch again and feel with the palms of my hands over the area of the worst staining. Something gives a little under my hand. The iron hatch over the refuse-chute is heavy and resists my efforts. I let my arms fall to my sides. I am exhausted; my arms ache. So too does my neck on which my head, thrown back at an awkward angle, is being put under undue strain. I try the hatch again. Again I feel the force of its personality, as if it were wrestling against me. One more go. I have managed to push it to one side. I heave myself into the open. At least I can make out a small square of sky, but I am not yet free, alas. I am in a courtyard with three high stone walls topped with an arrangement of iron spokes, a fourth wall composed of a padlocked iron grille. What a suspicious lot these Swiss are! I wonder whether they are more intent upon keeping *out* intruders or keeping guests *in*.

There is no way that I can scale these walls. I shall try climbing the grille. I place my feet carefully on the heads of rounded flowers and nicely curled foliage that make up the design at the foot of the grille and lift myself into the branches of the trees that spread right and left to form the bars. Having reached the top, I can rest. I curl myself to fit into one of the nests of the storks in the crown of the iron forest.

I drop soundlessly on to the snow. I am free. What

exhilaration I feel! But not for long. I am pierced by freezing cold: my face is pricked and scoured, my feet numb, my fingers crippled. I am colder than fear. Suddenly I realize that I am clad in my pyjamas. I say 'my', but surely these are not mine? These are striped flannel, not cream silk. Were it feasible, I would turn back for warm clothing. But it is not.

I look forward on a land subdued. Junket white. Horizontal but not flat. I glide along a treacherous path on which no previous individual has passed since the monstrous cold wave broke over civilization, freezing everything beneath it. The ghostly white that spreads itself across the lands confers no brightness. Its purpose is to shroud. I notice the wind whining. I suspect that shortly it will wail, threaten the air and burst into a commanding rage. This is the way of the wind and the air, in its dread of it, is standing stiff as shock watching, as I am lifted off my feet, shaken about and hurled to the edge of the pit. Now I am cold as death. Only the trickle of warm urine making its way affectionately down my thigh gives me the hope that my inner organs remain warmly supple.

If I am to stay alive in this cold I must not sleep.

For lack of any alternative, I submit to the wind and lie looking down into the bowels of the pit. I do not dare to try to get to my feet. I know that any slightly stronger gust will dispatch me to the depths from which there would surely be no escape. In which event I am in no doubt as to what my fate would be. I had heard from a man with a pack on his back, walking the world in his room, what had happened to others when Boreas, Caecias, Argestes and Thrascias combined to wreak revenge. They swept up men of no account and hurled them into the pit, followed by rats. The rats ate the carcasses and then one another and the few left were consumed by flies. Only then was the air made clean again, free to be blown about. If only the wind would subside, now. If only I were able to climb to the top of the mountain, then I could save the world! I turn my face to get the mountain in my sight. I see torrents twisting like serpents, hungry for human blood. Now the mist is rolling in on giant waves. The sky is merging with the ground. A sort of opaque, white darkness conceals the limitless silence.

Sabine sent me here to rest, to renew myself. She spoke of the rare birds which breed here, of unique vegetation, of herbs and spices unknown elsewhere, of pure air, of peace and quiet. Most of my adult life, I have allowed myself to submit to Sabine. It has never crossed my mind that she might be wrong about anything, or have ulterior motives. I preferred to have confidence in her than question her. But when I look back, I can see that she and my customers really did expect too much of me: greater and greater feats of endurance, never less than perfection, absolute reliability, no swings of mood. I could never dare to fall short as a chef or I would lose my reputation: my stars. Sabine could not have weathered such misfortune. And customers do not give one a second chance. But I have failed as a man. As a man I am neither rich nor successful. I am neither desired nor respected. I have adopted a prone position, feeling vanquished in advance of any effort I might have considered making. The only way open to me, leading to a situation in which I could achieve mastery over myself was if, like Vatel, I took my life into my hands and finished it off. But I doubt I have the skill. Even Vatel had to fall against his sword *three* times. And do I have his courage? I think not. Yet I feel I have lived long enough. I am fifty-five. Fifty-five years are quite enough to have achieved more than personal mediocrity. But that is the curse of my class. And anyone can see from looking at me and listening to me from where I hail: not from a respected class but a respectable one. When I get back to my knives, perhaps. That is a consoling thought. I would at least have control over something. Complete control, even. Now, there's an ambition to realize. And the nourishment of eternal sleep. Nor would my control end there. I would insist, I would lay down the rites to be followed. I would rule from the grave with penalties for those who did not adhere to my wishes: a cardboard coffin, cremation, my ashes to be interred with the bones of Carême. And the end of Les Coteaux.

It is not generally understood that a goaler can be loving and sympathetic, even beautiful, but none the less a goaler. Sabine was one such. She made herself invaluable but clanged like a chatelaine with a key to every lock and a lock for every purpose. If I had tried to wrest something of my autonomy from her, she would have loosened her grip, thrown down the keys and robbed me of it by insisting I take it all.

Sabine told me that when she was a child she had been convinced that she was reserved for something grand and powerful. Before she could even read and write, Dr Widmer gave her a magnet. She would sit for hours on end, transfixed by the patterns she could make in iron filings by passing her little horseshoe under the tray on which she had scattered them. It was an early lesson in how to run Les Coteaux, and me.

Sabine has the hauteur of a tulip, proud and impressive. By comparison with her head held high, mine droops like my dead member.

My mind is filled with the shapes of death and dying. I pick my way through the trackless wastes. The stones beneath my feet are rotting. I am alone and in danger. The hail that pelts, the wind that is raging, the ice-wet

59

punishments have only my skin to tear to shreds, my eyes to blind and my blood to congeal. I am insubstantial. The storm rips through me regardless, for I am as nothing.

This is the absolute death of the stillborn. Is this the end of the world or the world before it begins? Such uncontrollable circumstances render Sabine's decisions on my behalf pathetic.

I must resolve not to kill myself on a day of impatience with Sabine.

I can make out two categories of people here. Of course there may be more and I have not yet come across them. But of the two categories I have detected, there are among them those who seem to be in residence permanently, who may well have been born here, and others who are just visiting. I cannot explain to myself how I have come to this conclusion, except to say that I may have registered their status from the manner in which they move about. Some dawdle, some crawl, some drag themselves along the ground on their backsides, swinging on crutches, groping sightless along the walls, their eyes stitched shut with barbed wire, hovering on sticks, creeping, tottering, shuffling along prescribed lines. There are those who stand stationary, motionless. I have taken them for stone effigies. All are maimed, whether by life itself or by their failed efforts to escape, I cannot say. Liberty is a powerful assailant. These people do not communicate at any length. I have overheard some speak but it is invariably to themselves. The others, the visitors, have illnesses of addiction: raging jealousy, obsession, a desire to consume ever increasingly, selfishness, imperiousness. They appear physically intact, but one or two have mislaid their memories, others their minds. At some point, they believe they stand a chance of getting out if they make progress. But I am pretty sure they cannot be much concerned about leaving, for they make no attempts at escape. They talk at great length, not to one another but in the presence of others. They have stories to tell. This must be a consolation. For although I have not mislaid my memory or my mind, I have no story to tell. Nothing of interest. But when I get out of this place, when finally I escape, then I shall have a story to tell.

I am much relieved to have been given a table to myself in the dining-room. I am the only guest seated alone, well apart from the others. I have decided that I shall always walk to my table before the others enter, and leave when they have gone. That way I shall avoid arousing curiosity. I find that when I enter the dining-room, I notice the noise of dishes and pans and distant voices coming from the kitchen. Then, when the dining-room fills, the noise becomes like that in a concert hall before the conductor appears and the instrumentalists are tuning up: generalized sound without meaning. On the one hand I find this consoling, for I do not want the ideas of others to impinge on mine. On the other hand, the lack of meaning can be disconcerting to someone who like myself favours clarity, and so I have taken to throwing my ear on to a particular table to listen to the story being told.

'Why did I marry Geoff? Well, silly, he was the only one to ask. And I'd had an unfortunate start. There'd been a dance at the village hall, in aid of something Mother approved and so she said it was all right for me to go. Anyhow my brother and his girl were going. I had a nice dress, green rayon with a little lace collar, if I remember rightly. There was this young man asked me to dance. I said I couldn't and he said neither could he. So he drew up a chair and sat down by my side. It wasn't easy talking because of the noise of the band and the young people larking about. But I told him I was taking care of Mother and he told me he'd been at work five years and asked me if I'd like to partake of a sausage roll and something to wash it down with and so we got up and went to the back where they'd set up the trestle-table with a nice cloth. You know the sort of thing. And we stood there. He worked at Mudie's, it turned out, the stationers. Said he'd be manager before he was thirty-five. Told me ever so many things about his mum and dad and how he cycled all over Oxfordshire of a Sunday. He loved nature, you see, because he'd been born in Manchester. Asked if he could escort me home. I explained I was with Reg and Phyllis, but if he liked. He held my arm along the lane, and when we got to the gate he kissed me good-night. I felt, well, it's hard to explain how I felt. I've not felt like that since. It was a nice feeling, but quite upsetting. I had to tell him I'd best go in right away.

'That must've been the Saturday. On the Monday, after I'd come in from the shop, I found a bunch of cow-slips on the doorstep. There was a little card with my name on it and on the back "Thanks". I thought it was a peculiar message, in the circumstances, but one can never be sure. What could he be thanking me for? But it was a nice gesture on his part, and I'd enjoyed the evening. I was struck how prettily he'd put the bunch together with the tall ones in the middle and the short ones all round, and the whole thing tied with grasses.

'I went to bed that night feeling quite important. I thought maybe he'd write to me. I didn't like to write to him at Mudie's, you know how one doesn't, and I didn't know the address of his lodgings. Well, I didn't hear anything on the Tuesday nor the Wednesday and I knew Thursday was half-day and I thought maybe he'd cycle over and I'd thank him then. But he didn't.

'I was washing up Mother's lunch on the Saturday, two weeks later, when Mrs Hodges from the Donkey Welfare dropped in. "Oh," I said, "nice to see you, Mrs Hodges. Will you have a cup of tea?" I dried my hands on my apron and took her into the sitting-room and we sat over tea and Bourbons and during our little talk Mrs Hodges asked me if I'd found the cowslips. "Mrs Abercrombie was ever so grateful to you for delivering her order, she asked me what I thought you might like as a little thank-you and I said Janet loves flowers more than anything in the world. Well, she said, that's easy then. And she got Doris to get out into the field and pick some."

'Come to think of it, I've never been able to look at a cowslip since.'

I find the banality of this overhearing reassuring. Surely there can be nothing to fear from a place where such a woman has come for a rest. And then I spot Sir Archibald Clary, his appearance unpleasing as ever, his skin coley grey-white, his white hair nicotine stained. He is enticing a crowd of down-and-outs through the door, appealing to them to join him at his table. Now seated, he is asking his guests to leave the ordering of the meal to him. 'I shall order the finest.' And I hear him speak of caviare, of *foie gras* and his favourite dish of all, 'A swan with a *farce* of dried fruit and nuts'.

Slobbering, vomiting – for the food is excessively rich and the poor unfortunates so ill-nourished they would have had difficulty keeping down thin gruel – they remain seated for hours. They lick the last crumbs from their plates, and then the table. Sir Archibald is solicitousness itself. He rises from his seat and goes round the table asking his guests in turn if they have enjoyed the meal. He wipes their mouths. He takes their fingers and dips them in the scented water of the finger-bowls and pats them dry on the damask napkins. Now, helping each off his chair, he presents one of the men with a bill. I know it will amount to an average life's wages. 'Until every one of you has settled your debt, you will be locked in that cupboard over there!' I watch as he whips thirty men and women into the cupboard. Tears of mirth trickle down Sir Archibald's face, he is holding on to his sides, he is whacking his thigh in a frenzy of delight. The thirty down-and-outs press into a cupboard designed for silver, cutlery and glass. They are being pressed like flowers between the pages of a book.

'Ah!' Sir Archibald is sighing, rubbing his hands, 'A very good job done. That'll teach you to expect something for nothing!'

And now I see Lady Clary at his side. 'Or is it that these individuals are mentally wanting?' she inquires, quite gently. 'For were they in full possession of their senses, would they not have avoided poverty? Perhaps we should treat the poor as we treat the sick: lock them in houses of detention. Then we'd not be forced to set eyes on them or even think about them. There are too many second-class citizens these days. We don't need them: we have machines.' And turning to the closed cupboard she shouts: 'D'you imagine we are here for you, to provide you with food and shelter? You are here for us. Remember that! This is the first-class compartment and you have second-class tickets. You purport to be hungry. I have no doubt you are, but that hardly entitles you to a place at our table!'

Lady Clary's committee has ruled that the ill are possessed. By demons. Society, the committee insists, must be reformed. The sick infect the world for the rest of us. (Us? Which of 'us'?) Lady Clary has taken the trouble to identify the symptoms of the possessed and the treatment from which they might benefit. 'The mad do not

64

feel cold, pain, humiliation or degradation. They are evil and should be whipped, branded, cold-showered and eventually starved. They should be confined to the sewers, for they are waste men.' No wonder they tend to hide. I have found them everywhere in the dark corners, under the floor-boards, under piles of old rags, in dustbins.

My ears are filled with the muffled cries of the prisoners of the world in their manacles and chains.

Should I sit in the public rooms or shall I be called upon to contribute to the conversation? They might want a story from me. No one has approached me so far. My history, my views, my plans for the future are of no interest, it would seem. And I prefer to subsist on the lees of conversation. Sometimes, someone will indicate the existence of an unoccupied chair at his side, no doubt because he requires a listener. But not today. Not now. And I pass through the door, across the foyer and into the corridor, then down the white line, pursued by the malodorous reality of public life.

Through a crack in the lavatory door I can see a woman retch and vomit, her head hung well over the pan. 'God be with me! Gentle Jesus! Help me!' She is half covered by an old, beige blanket, her crushed body like a porridge saucepan left unwashed. Under her flows a stream of her waste. She falls back unconscious, her mouth streaked with yellow strands of half-digested food.

I must have passed out. The next thing I knew was the sound of tambourines. Down the line, the white line, in Indian file, small people are moving on all fours. 'Where are you going?' No one raises his head or glances in my direction. No one makes a sound. Are they all deaf? Are they asleep? I feel I should not have posed the question.

They are to be held in chains, clapped in pillories. They will suffer strangulation, flaying and decapitation. They will try to escape the terror but will succeed only in turning

65

over the tables against which they dash themselves in an effort to leave the room.

The snow screams under my feet as if in agony. Great tower blocks of ice with impenetrable entrances and exits rise at regular intervals into the distance. These are the solid frozen crematoria for lost souls. I have never before seen so many or such lofty monuments. I pick my way respectfully across the agonized ground, guilty to be the source of its present pain. I sense that there is more to suffering than I had thought.

It is the spectre of infinity that accompanies me as I try to regain my room. I climb more and more stairs, I set out along corridors that are unending, that twist and turn, that branch off into flights of narrow stairs which open on to more corridors with doors and windows whose views always overlook the interior, rooms large and small, crammed with objects, people and atmospheres. Sometimes a tangible emptiness. I can see a crowd of men gathering, peering through a window. A guide in a grey mackintosh and sou'wester is reciting a commentary: 'This is the fate of the barren women. None has made a copy of herself. None has anything to launch on the river of time. Each will be obliterated, here, shortly. See: they are not all old, but all are withered, dying before flowering. They are without desire. None has been gripped by passion, has offered herself to another for his delight and satisfaction.' I watch as he taps the window with his stick. The light responds by going out. The little group moves on as one. I hear one say: 'I knew a man whose wife was barren. He yearned for a son. He belonged to a mystical sect whose faith in the fertility of the sign of the fish was absolute. Into the pram, a mere box on wheels that his wife had installed in their hall, for the infant she failed to conceive, my friend placed a carp, dressed in a bonnet and long night-shirt. Every afternoon he left work early to come home and wheel the fish into the town square where he solicited the admiration of the tradesmen and women.'

I should have had a son to call Antoine.

They are administering far too many tablets. I know they are. This morning I put the three in my mouth, took a draught from the glass of water I was handed, and managed to conceal the beastly things at one side of my mouth, between my back gum and cheek. Then, when I was alone, I spat them out. But I would have preferred not to deceive. Why don't I have the courage to refuse, to say 'NO, I won't!'? There are worse dangers, that's why. If I don't take the pills, there may be worse to come. I have seen the torture-chamber. When I say 'seen', I mean that out of the corner of my eye, through a half-open door, I have seen the men come to tattoo the patients with their crimes – or is it their illnesses? – and sort them for treatment. Treatment! Now, there's a word.

I wish I could close my ears. Their voices are like knives scraping metal. And their laughter is levelled against me. It is piercing me with the force of a bullet. Little slivers of shrapnel are lodging themselves under my skin. They are laughing to split my sides. Yet what can there be about me to evoke such merriment?

They are speaking of an unsettling discovery they have made. Under their hallucinogens they find within themselves every sign and symptom of psychosis. 'Insanity is universal!' they laugh, 'Insanity is ever-present!' they add, victoriously. I determine to walk backwards to avoid this future, and to concentrate on learning to close my ears, for I am hearing too much at once: whispers, innuendoes

67

and puns. I would prefer the company of the soundless.

They are wearing uniforms. I cannot make out whether they are doctors or engineers, whether they administer to men or machines. If they are to be my masters, I must learn how to despise them. Just because there are no notices to instruct me as to what to do is no reason for them to mock me.

I happen to be rather hungry. I would like a piece of buttered toast with a single portion of Oxford marmalade, but I dare not ask for it. I might be thought to be making difficulties. I may be able to avoid detection if I do not make difficulties. I cannot eat the food in the dining-room. It is disgusting, all white and soft. Unidentifiable for the most part. It fails to appeal to sight, touch, taste or smell. These people do not have a clue. If I am to ingest poison, what am I to evacuate? This reversal is an abuse of nature. And I who have always been so prudent. Anyhow, to complain I would need my voice and I am not at all sure I can still speak. When last did I utter the merest sound? I cannot remember doing so since being here. I should test out my voice to see whether it is still in my throat and available for use. But I would feel such a fool, testing. When men are kept chained prisoners for long periods, their legs forget how to answer the commands of their will. I do not want to forget how to cough.

Sabine knows full well that I do not like change. At any price. Why has she ignored this? I like everything to be the same, day after day, week after week. Nor have I ever sought excitement. She knows that. She knows that perfectly well. Once I have discovered a mode of being that suits me, I like to regard it as permanent. Why forgo it? I am not searching for the unattainable. I know what I have to achieve and I have achieved it: four stars.

She sent me here so that I would stop re-creating Carême's pastry masterpieces. She thought they were old

68

hat. She could not bear his Turkish pavilion or the ruins of a rotunda with fountain (with strips of angelica for the water). She was tired of mocking me to no effect for my version of Carême's *meringue gâteau* in the shape of a hedgehog, for his roman helmets in marzipan and harps and lyres in spun sugar. She sent me here for old spite's sake.

Walking resolutely in search of escape into the open, along a corridor that is familiar for being the same as all the others, yet unrecognizable for being identical, I see behind a glass screen a space that appears to be a gymnasium: bare floor-boards, wall-bars, ropes slung from the ceiling and a few pieces of free-standing equipment upon which to impale oneself. Here is where they leave their repressions stored in lockers and enter the wide-open space of exhibitionism. Thirty male mannequins from the windows of department stores, some old, bent and wrinkled, their flesh whey-coloured, others no more than children, their flesh pink, smooth and lithe. Such is the silence, all I can hear is the ringing of the blood in my own ears. Yet I can see that the mouths of the men are exploding with noise and those of the youngsters seeping with desolation. All faces are wrung with pain and terror. All eyes uncomprehending. Some of the figures are adopting an all-fours position, and stamping rhythmically like bored horses. Some have started to kick out at their fellows. The strong are actually pulling the limbs of the weak in an effort to detach them. There's nothing I can do from here. I am impotent. And I know what is in store, for I have already located where severed limbs are discharged. I must get away, there is nothing I can do to help. I must walk faster. Much faster. I refuse to assist at a disembowelling.

69

But this is an endless corridor. However hard I try to avoid glancing in that direction, I cannot help seeing what is going on behind the glass screens to my left and right. They are setting up target practice. Each of the despised wears a white moon over the heart so that when the Jew, the black or the crippled is to be shot, the marksmen will not waste their bullets. I see the marksmen line up in accordance with their prejudices. I must find a way not to look. I shall take the door marked NO ADMITTANCE where the rich are making plans for a tournament. Convicts are to be thrown to the crocodiles. I am close to the organizers. I can hear what they are saying. I must remonstrate with them, but I have no voice. They mock me by showing me their intentions. They are going to couple. Right there: before me. I turn my head and have to face the river turning from grey to red.

Heaps of soiled linen are spread like grease over the floor and piled high against the lacerated walls, bleeding damp. In the corner a naked derelict, unconscious in his incontinence, is coiled in a foetal position, his hands clasped between his thighs. I do not want to rouse him. This would involve me in communication. None the less, I approach, treading cautiously between the piles of linen to the nest he has made for himself. Writhing under the skin of his hairless limbs I can see tiny, whitish, ovoid bodies: larvae feasting. I am transfixed. I cannot move from my ghastly vantage-spot. This man's flesh is being consumed while he sleeps. Little by little a cloud of common flies is rising into the air, hovering there, as if to pay its final respects. I try to turn, to move away. Now the cloud of flies moves with me. Some are making for my mouth. I can feel them buzzing at my gums. It is disgusting and I try spitting them out, but every time I open my mouth

70

to get rid of them, others enter. Now they are attacking my eyes and nose. I shall pull my jacket over my head. Now they are invading me at the waist. . . .

I seem to have no control over where to go or where to be. I am being swept along in the slipstream of uncertainty. I cannot be sure which of the events I am caught up in precedes the other. Each event seems to happen simultaneously with another and another, and my frustration arises out of the difficulty of putting overlapping experiences in the correct order. In the normal way, even though I lack imagination, I know (or is it that I sense?) the future at which to take aim. I notice time passing and how what I inquired of yesterday may have its answer today. Here, now, nothing follows on what preceded it. What act of mine could have precipitated this state of being? Of what is this the consequence?

Is it night or day? Is it that the lights have gone out or I am unseeing? I feel movement underfoot. This could be a floe that has drifted from the sea. Or an avalanche. Something huge is sliding towards me. I hear it approaching. It is about to engulf me. The sensation is not altogether unpleasant, even momentarily comforting. Now I remember: I am alone, lonely engulfed in corpulence. This is no nourishing breast, no enfolding arms, but a land mass stealthily squeezing the life out of me. Will it be that I freeze or starve to death, my life whited out by this mountainous, inert chalkiness? If I were strong (if I were a Samson of a man) I would spread my arms and push back the imploding walls. But I have never made physical fitness a goal. Fitness freaks make me sick, bore me to death. Why run faster to a place you do not want to reach? Why jump higher than your neighbour? But with all the exits sealed off and a keen desire to be free

71

of my situation, including the proximity of these people, I wish now that I had trained.

The attic skylights are overlaid with snow that deadens the light. This space is empty as hunger. Inhospitable. Had I a voice it would echo. There would be nothing but me answering myself with the question I pose.

I am wandering through empty places under the roof. Empty places that open on to other empty places until I reach a graveyard of once-cherished things: a fur coat decomposing in a corner, heaving with insect life; keyless pianos, their wires entangled in silence; rusting, bladeless lawn-mowers in a pool of their own oil; once-loved, forever discarded broken toys. I know that I am in peril of being swept up with this rubbish and disposed of in neglect.

Did Sabine admit or commit me to this hell? She was so sure I was pathologically anxious and feared I might be suicidal. She could not allow that between a feeling of anxiety and a death wish there might extend an infinity of disturbance that would respond to gentle treatment. A well-organized individual such as Sabine does not experience disturbance. She creates it in others. Anxiety by proxy, they call it. She pushed me a dish too far, but only on to the lowest rung of the ladder of disturbance. Around me, here, circle those who have attained higher rungs, poor sods! What precipitated their incarceration? I never knew that there existed inns for people who want 'out'....

Why has that man been manacled to a radiator? I know it is a *cold* radiator and he is wearing just a few rags attached to him with string. I have seen him before. Every day he gets thinner. His legs protrude from the remnants of the night-shirt rags and I can see they are just bone. His fingers are the same. He is nothing more than a skeleton with a little skin stretched across his skull. And he can groan. How he groans! He'll be dead soon. I would have liked to bring him back to life but he was always

72

too far gone. I saw how a tube had been inserted in his nose and thick, white liquid pumped into him. But if it had been intended to nourish him through his stomach, it was an ill-conceived idea, because he had no stomach. The fluid simply poured out of him seconds after it poured in.

I wish I knew the time. I am accustomed to keeping to a routine. I would feel more relaxed if I knew the hour and what I should be doing. I have lost all track of time. That is not to say there are no clocks. There is one here in the foyer. But it is of a design with which I am not familiar. The sort of clock I have been used to consulting has two hands that move around a face, pointing at numbers. The clock here has a phallus that penetrates the numbers, themselves gold-rimmed orifices that open to admit the member, close to contain it, then eject it to press forward to the next vent. On the hour the swollen member emits its seed, which falls on to the chimes. But I am not convinced that the five ringing chimes I hear were to be followed by six, or preceded by four.

On more than one occasion, Sabine remarked that I was not like other men in that I had no need of entertainment. But she was not altogether correct in this judgement. I like the cinema and the theatre. I keep away from both for particular reasons. So far as the cinema is concerned, my fear is to find myself sitting next to the viewer with an outsize bag of sweets for sucking and nuts for crunching, or with hair flattened with foul-smelling unction. I could never muster the courage to get up from my seat and choose another. As for the theatre, audience participation is fashionable these days. I am haunted by the prospect of being addressed from the stage or, worse, being drawn on to the stage. I can imagine nothing worse. In any case, as like as not, I would have selected the

73

play in order to enjoy witnessing experiences I would never have to endure personally. What would be the point of being drawn into them?

I have always been aware of life's danger zones. I prefer to avoid them. But I could never admit as much to Sabine. I could not show myself weak, miserable or stupid to her. It would mean letting her down. And the terrible fact is that she would show indulgence, with lurking disappointment. I could not bear that.

Something else I make a point of avoiding: public lavatories. I make it a rule never to be taken short. Once, when I was visiting a provincial city, I was obliged to use the lavatory at a railway station. I was just lowering myself on to the seat when I noticed that a piece of paper was being pushed through a slit in the fabric of the wall. I felt violated. I leapt off the seat, leaving my business unfinished. I ignored the note; I did not want to learn its contents. And I was furious to have had my innocent pleasure interrupted. For me the evacuation of my bowels is one of life's greatest delights. It is free, it is legal, it lacks struggle.

'Our neighbour, Mr Holman, was not happy with his wife and because no other solution proposed itself, he murdered her. Naturally he was anxious not to be discovered in his crime. He had a programme of work to complete. He took his wife on holiday to an island in the Pacific and drowned her. Since they had lived an isolated life for a quarter of a century, no one among us so much as inquired after Mrs Holman when Mr Holman arrived back.

'His *Dictionary of Fleas* was due for publication within three years, but he found himself surprisingly unstimulated by the work involved. Unexpectedly morose, he realized

74

that the absence of Maud was as depressing as her presence had been. Images of her struggle to avoid his determined grasp of her, as he pushed her deeper and deeper under the water and held her fast, surfaced on his mind and left him with an indelibly etched image of his wife's imploring expression.

'When I was a child, we lived in a village half-way between Ely and Cambridge. My father was the rector of St Mary's-on-the-Fen at Elton. In those days it was customary for gentlemen of the road, as they dignified themselves, to call at rectories for food and, in inclement weather, shelter. My father was most un-Christian about this. I remember my mother remonstrating with him. "Cedric," she would say, "what d'you suppose Our Lord would have done?" And she would dart off to slice bread, find clothes and direct the tramp to the garden shed.

'I learnt years later that my father hadn't started off life mean and inhospitable but had become so through a single experience in which he had been duped. He never got over it.

'He was a curate living on a very small stipend somewhere in the Midlands when he regularly dropped what little he had into the greasy old hat of a beggar who stationed himself at the lych-gate from ten in the morning until sundown. The man was dressed in rags, was unshaven and dirty and seemed confused. Father would ask him sometimes where he lived and how he made out in the cold, but the old man seemed unable to string together coherent sentences. Father would allow him to sit in the church, out of the rain and cold, and would bring him his own food to eat and collect clothes for him. This state of affairs went on for about three years until the third winter, which was a particularly harsh one. There was snow on the ground for three weeks and the temperature at night fell to well below freezing and Father

75

worried about the man. One day as dusk fell he followed the tramp and watched as he took a key from his pocket and let himself into the basement of a fine Georgian house in the most desirable part of town. Father was astonished but not yet suspicious. Wishing to satisfy himself that the man had regular shelter, he followed him from time to time over several months and each night saw him enter the same house. Then he did become suspicious and looked into the case.

'The man's name was Bateman, and as a child from a destitute family living in a caravan in the Forest of Dean he had gone to work in a brick factory near the forest and later in the Midlands. Eventually he had become the owner of that factory and when he sold it he put some of his fortune into gold bars and the rest in the bank. He was not mean with his wife but he loathed her, and just as soon as his sons left home he decamped from the main part of the house to the basement, leaving his wife to occupy the rest of the house. He provided her with regular payments to run the house as it had been run ever since he had become affluent: the house was heated, there was abundant food and there were servants. He received regular statements from the bank which showed that his finances were in good order, that he had more income than he and his wife spent, and that his gold bars were safe, intact in the deposits.

'But Mr Bateman's conscience was troubled. First, he felt guilty that alone of all his brothers and sisters only he had done well financially and had never helped the others. Secondly, he was aware that the very circumstances which had led to the poverty of his parents, the greed of the rich, he himself perpetuated in that he had prospered at the expense of his workers. He greatly feared that one day he would be revenged.'

They were all going to tell their stories. It would be

rude of me to leave the foyer now. I shall sit while the next one is told, and unless it helps me to calculate what to expect next, I shall slip out during the clapping.

'Once upon a time there lived a queen who was heartily sick of all her subjects falling over themselves to flatter her. "I shall give my kingdom to the first man to tell me the truth about myself," she told a packed audience gathered to pay her homage. None believed her. Queens have reasons and so do we, they argued, and ours is not to reason theirs. However, a subject who had been living in a cave in the most far-flung outpost of her kingdom, and had happened upon the audience by chance, and attended only because of the beer and sandwiches, took the queen to one side.

'"You are acting most foolishly!" he told her.

'"I shall give you my kingdom!"

'"No one could rule as unjustly as you, my sovereign!"

'"You shall have my kingdom!"

'"Despite the undoubted fact that you are without exception the ugliest, smelliest, most neurotic of all the inhabitants of this land, your inclinations are admirable."

'"All of it shall be yours!"

'"None the less, and whatever your fine qualities, there is nothing I should like less than to share my life with you."

'"I am yours!"'

I have no story to relate. Was I invited to this party? Had I accepted or refused the invitation? Have we all been abandoned here? I wonder whether this possibility has occurred to the others? Some may want to go home but have no homes and are here because they are incapable of grasping this piece of logic. But in that event, why are their hands restrained in canvas gloves, separately and placed one on top of the other and tied up? That must be why I am here: because I do not understand how one situation proceeds from another.

77

They appear not to see me. Should I call attention to myself? 'Look! Look! Over here. Look at me. I'm here!' But no one turns his head. I remember it was the same at school. But then it was a game. A boy or girl was *chosen* to be ignored. It was often me. I was stared through, my chair was pulled from under me, my plate cleared away before I had finished eating. I was wiped out. But this is not a game. I sense it derives from incuriousness rather than hostility. And who knows better than I that indifference is harder to bear than hatred?

'You have no close male friends!' Sabine would say. 'Oh yes I have! A close, dear, *dead* friend!' And she would pull a face. Yet were it not for Carême, where would *she* be? I cannot imagine any living friend would have been as generous to me as he had been. And it is not as if I have ever complained of being lonely. I am not lonely. I have my staff; I have my wife. My work requires my absolute obedience to my master and my staff's to me. Sabine provides the setting. Anything more in my life would be a distraction.

There is far too much to distract me here. There is chaos. Loud, vicious words hurled at the walls are bouncing off like so many cricket balls. They must belong to tales of battle. Now the walls are heaving, breathing in and out to absorb the noise. I risk being ingested. They are like a giant amoeba that is altering its shape to fold itself about me.

Who are the men slicing off the top of the children's heads? Some hold on to the lids and invite others to peer into the cavities. Hands dripping blood lift out the brains and replace them with sawdust. I turn my gaze on to the mouths of these unfortunates. I have never seen tooth-less and tongueless mouths before. It is as if someone had sliced a rubber ball from ear to ear. When these children ate they could only have slobbered. I think back to what mouths once meant to me: the possibility of a flow of words of approbation, not to mention sensitive taste-buds.

'There was once a wife who imagined her health was poor. Her husband sought the best in the land to tend her. "My kidneys are not quite right," she announced. "I shall make an appointment for you to consult Sir Owen Oppens. He is the best (and therefore the most expensive) in the land. But tell me," the husband inquired, "what is it precisely that worries you about the functioning of your kidneys?" The wife did not reply but threw him a glance of great skill. For years she had been practising that look, one that said: "Something very serious is wrong with me but I shall spare you the details, and am I not still in my suffering the loveliest young woman you have ever wanted to embrace?" The woman settled back on the throne of her perfection and smiled with satisfaction. But then, on reflection, her smile turned to a scowl. Had she married with less profit than she had foreseen? Had she imagined her husband would spend a lifetime ratifying her opinions?'

And now a group has formed. They are all talking about me. I know this although I cannot hear what they are saying. I know too that the books they carry under their arms are filled with tales about me. I myself have looked into those books. I can testify to the fact that they are pure fiction. I don't know where they could have got their stories from. The group is dispersing but the damage is done. They detain one another in little conversations but move on and away. One raises a hat, another waves a glove. Some shake hands. And yet in these listless, injured and hapless people resides great cruelty.

There is no point in attempting an objection. I would

not be believed. Anyhow, if I try my voice I shall only discover it has gone.

From the landing window I see that the white ground and the white sky have risen and fallen into an impenetrable fog that has come to rest against the windowpanes. I have to escape. But I need to rest before attempting another break-out.

I find myself looking out on a land undulating in frozen, glass waves that glisten yellow under an unambitious sun. I have observed from my window that the sun never rises high but hangs wan at about forty-five degrees. Something is rattling in the wind. Now it blows a fistful of ice slivers into my face. As I raise my hand to my stinging cheek, my bleeding eyes, an uncontrolled gust hurls me into an irreducible landscape. Algid! In the far distance I hear a rock fall. It echoes like tumbrils over cobbles. I think of starving men who eat the lice off their bodies. I am desperate for food and shelter. I try standing upright. I can breathe only if I walk backwards; the wind is suffocating. All about me is the sound of cracking and groaning: the world being ground between millstones.

Under the floor-boards the dead kneel. Their hair is three feet long and their toe- and finger-nails three inches long. The owls that had come to carry off the children died here, too. Some of the adults had been partly eaten by the hungry children. The torment of unappeased hunger hangs in the fetid air.

I have entered a room in which all that remains is what is left when it is empty: habits, repeated jokes and little deceptions.

The days have closed in on one another in a continuous sentence. In the foyer the story-telling continues unbroken.

'I was passing along Floral Street, it was winter. I watched a young man without means, who had been squatting in the doorway of a betting shop, raise himself on his head and stay in that position for several seconds before resuming his sheltered corner. The street was deserted and in semi-darkness. I thought to myself, fifty pence given to that young man is fifty pence wasted. He will put it on the three-thirty at Kempton Park and that will be that. On reaching the opera-house, I saw another, similarly disadvantaged young man. He was of a very different character, however. He selected a portion of well-lit pavement, brushed it free of dirt with a rolled newspaper, placed his can before him and rose quickly on his head and wiggled his feet in front of the well-heeled crowd. That young man, I told myself, will go far. Fifty pence dropped into his (clean) cap will not find its way to Mecca but will gather with other coins to provide him with a hot meal. With a hot meal in his stomach, he will feel the urge to search for work. And so I dropped him a coin and felt thoroughly reassured.'

Sabine said of the new bourgeoisie that it does not aspire to knowledge and wisdom, only to money.

'I am reminded of the words of a traveller in an outlandish corner of Turkey, who took lodgings in a village in the mountains for just one night, although he had originally counted on spending two or three. The reason for his precipitous departure was this. Sitting by the fountain at the centre of the little group of houses that constituted the main square at A, he noticed a small barefoot boy with one eye on the right of his face and no second eye on the left. The child was frightfully thin and had a limp. He stopped at the traveller's feet to examine his shoes. A profound sadness emanated from the child. As the traveller's hand delved deep in his pocket for some coins, a woman appeared at an open doorway clutching a baby at her breast. She spat into the dirt. Addressing the traveller she shouted: "Just another mouth to feed, sir! Another bastard! He should've died at birth."'

In our world the poor are worthless, or they would be rich.

'Many years ago, when men were more inclined than they are today to consider such matters, a group of religious thinkers gathered together to discuss God's purpose. He had created the world in order to be able to differentiate between the righteous and the wicked. The absolutely evil world that had been in his mind to create, he set aside: no righteous man could emerge from pure evil. Thus it was that he created laws that govern nature, human society and history, laws that only the most devoted pietist could confront and overcome the trials. God, they said, was an examiner. All his laws are inimical to human desire, making it almost impossible for us to be good. At some level of our being we are conscious of this and we have invented guilt, a self-inflicted suffering that the penitent among us pay for our pleasure. The trouble is, and God did not foresee this, that sin in our minds is related to pleasure and to righteousness.'

A man is seated at a roll-top desk writing down what he wants to forget. He is surrounded by piles of crisp black, the consistency of onion skin. He picks up the telephone: 'Cancel that appointment for Monday! I find Mondays too yellow to bear. They agitate me. Make it Tuesday, when it's green.' Should I draw his attention to the fact that the telephone lines are down? Had they been working, I would have rung Sabine. I would not have sounded cross with her or upset, I would simply have requested her to sort things out so that I might leave.

82

The man writing is clearly oblivious of the man close to him orating. This is surprising, since this man cannot move because his head, the size of a normal torso, has no neck and rests on flippers and anyone might wonder how he manages life and might want to be given an explanation. His learning is extraordinary and his eloquence equal to it. The words he proclaims are not his own, however, but are culled from the greatest books ever written. He has already recited the works of Goethe in their entirety. Now he is embarking on Homer. This is evidently his space. He is here always. People come and people go but he can be relied upon to be *in situ* reporting the thoughts of others.

Above his wisdom the air is filled with grunting, roaring, laughter and tears. I want to get my back against something solid, but as I lean against the wall it shifts and I fall. The floor is awash with filth. I am shut up with monsters and cannot get out. Something horrible is tugging at my leg. Something child-sized without a face. I draw back in horror. I put out my hand, hoping to catch myself as I fall towards a wall. My hand is lost in the consistency of dough. My arm follows. My whole body is being sucked in. I feel as if I have been digested by a rubber glove that stinks. Around me circle the children of fanatically religious parents: blessings to offer, angels for the heavenly court.

Above my head on a washing line babies are being hung out on meat hooks.

What am I doing sitting in this foyer among people who address one another but ignore me? Perhaps I am no more than my own idea, which no other has had and therefore cannot recognize. Solitude, once a condition I chose for myself, now fills me with the loneliness of childhood.

My heart is thumping. My pulse is beating irregularly. My palms are sweating. My mouth is parched. Should I perhaps be doing something I am not doing? Making a purchase? Taking my place in a queue? Visiting a hospital patient? 'You do very little,' Sabine used to say. 'Very little,' she would emphasize. 'But what you do, you do well!' And she seemed pleased.

On the shelves that line the walls Achilles' heels are ranged in serried rows. Every heel jolts under a rain of verbal barbs.

My feet do not so much as ruffle the sullen silence. It is as if nothing of me can make any impression. Why was I given life? I cannot remember a time when I wanted it particularly. Once or twice I imagined that, were the view to change, my own might. But I have always lived at right angles to the right angles that imprison me: the walls to my sides, the paving-stones beneath my feet. I can recall just one single occasion when I experienced a sensation greater than pleasure. It was a day like any other, I was bent over my saucepan, as I had been thousands of times before. But this was the first time I registered the lack of corners. I watched my sauce slosh unregulated by right angles. I observed that, absence of right angles notwithstanding, my sauce was safely contained within.

It occurs to me now that it never occurred to me then to please Sabine. When did I ever make her a present of my time? When after a few months of light courtship did I compliment her on her beauty, marvel at her intelligence, thank her for her organizational skills? I put her off with little emotions. I dissembled my feelings with one of Carême's fish dishes, or the shadow of a smile. Yet she never ceased to concern herself with my needs, said they were her *raison d'être*. (Once Sabine gets her teeth into something, she never bites off more than she can chew.) Too late now for regrets. I shall almost certainly never get back to Les Coteaux. The roads have been erased. There is no one to ask the way. All certainty has gone. All continuity. There is nothing to say the dark will end at dawn; the fact that it invariably did is no guarantee that it will invariably do so again. I can take nothing for granted. Nothing conforms. The thought that I may not get back now makes me feel ill, makes me ask whether I really want to get back. The heart has its reasons of which reason knows nothing. Maybe the body has, too, for I have lost the strength to attempt an escape. What the strong take from the weak, they never return.

What was it I did wrong? What was it that was so wrong as to deserve this? Try as I may, I cannot trace this consequence to its source.

Until I came here I always knew what to expect. Indeed, I never wanted surprises and never made room for them. When I added cream to my sauce, I knew the precise moment it would thicken my reduction. When I whisked my egg whites, I knew just when they would turn from soft to stiff peaks of airy foam. Everything proceeded logically, with the regularity and assurance of light at the turn of a switch. Here, not knowing what to expect, I no longer know myself.

Sabine robbed me of my certainty in turning on me to be inventive. It was not that she disparaged Carême. He was as much above her reproach as he was above mine. Yet she made me feel that his were not the dishes for the present, that they were outmoded, as if food were answerable to fashion. I fail to understand Sabine. In all else she is above fashion. As I have already mentioned, she wears the timeless creations of Worth and Patou. She

85

arranged Les Coteaux in the manner of the great Paris restaurants of the eighteenth century: starched damask, mahogany and brass fitments, classic crystal and silver. It was 'Dear Gastronome' who affected her, however hotly she may deny the fact. She is a *grande dame* used to slapping down impertinence.

I wonder: is there much inside me that Sabine has not 'arranged'? I hardly recognize myself except in my lack of initiative. Perhaps it is this very absence that made me unsuited to independence. I was born without it. Born into slavery for slavery.

I feel a mounting surge in my groin. I shall try to ignore it. It leads to the most terrible consequences: the Spread Eagle Cure. I have seen this in operation. Seen poor, confused men wander the corridors, their penises clasped in agitating hands, pounced on by men in white coats who strip them naked, throw them on their backs, take a limb each and stretch it at right angles to their bodies while a fifth throws buckets of icy water over them. It is not only in the outside world that sexual gratification is a sin.

I had no mistress. I did not dare. Maybe I shall take one here. Sabine will never find out.

A young man of exceptional beauty is staring unblinkingly at me as if he believes he can exercise control over me. I am not sure that he can but I have known someone unintentionally turn food rancid with a stare. I had to sack a *plongeur* for this very accomplishment. Later I learnt he had brought about a miscarriage in his mother. And so deeply was he affected by learning of a power over which he had no control, he blinded himself. I must take care.

'I shall go and bath!' the exquisite young man announces. 'When Socrates decided to take his life, before he took

86

the poison, he bathed. He wished to spare the women who would wash his dead body. His last, thoughtful words to his servant were "Crito! We owe a cock to Aesculapius. Do pay this debt!"'

So informed! So articulate! Are these his only powers or is it his beauty that fastens the adoring young woman to his side? (He is not addressing her but his reflection in the looking-glass. Passionately so.) In my mind's eye I have seized her, wrested her from where she is leaning against him. He has the poise and quiet of a Greek statue: timeless assurance. I am glad the lovely young woman cannot read my thoughts, for they are lascivious. I am glad that her intoxication with her brilliant, beautiful lover fastens her gaze unflinchingly upon him so that she will not notice me. Why should she notice me? Unlike him, loved and wanted, I am a mere accident, a mongrel cast out to fend for itself. (Bile is spilling from the corners of my mouth. It is starting to rot my lips.) But I am sure that someone in authority has seen through to my lust and will be planning a new 'treatment' for me. I shall probably be taken to pieces. I know about that treatment. Last night (was it last night?) I was spilt on to the floor with other guilty men and only narrowly escaped their fate. They had their arms removed. One had his head off. I heard someone say that I should have my face taken away for remoulding. I was not displeased. On the one hand this could have the advantage of confusing my tor-mentors. But then, on the other hand, would I recognize myself?

If this is a sanatorium, an inn for the ill, an asylum for the insane, and I really cannot say for sure and would not dare ask, the treatment is a riddle. I am being disorien-tated through terror. Were I to pluck up the courage to question the appropriateness of this treatment, I would certainly find myself both deaf and dumb. And I am pretty sure now that there is no escaping. I check the doors and windows. They are all barred, and tape seals the jambs. There are no keys in the keyholes. They are all on the belts of the janitors and others in charge. These facts are made worse by my knowing that not only have the roads and signposts gone from the outside, but all the lines of communication with the outside – radio, telephone – have been cut. The inmates are apathetic: they accept their fate, even enjoy it. They sit about telling pointless stories, acting parts they have assigned to themselves and each other, pretending to have eaten well, enjoyed a good night's sleep in this comfortable, safe environment. The most abused among them behave as if they felt they were *owed* the treatment they are receiving. I, too, am conscious of a deep, indelible feeling of remorse, but I do not remember what I did that was so evil I must reproach myself for it and submit to retribution. I suppose there is something and it is that something for which Sabine abandoned me here. But do I deserve to be made impotent in the face of the suffering of others, so that I cannot so much as raise a finger to help? And do I deserve the humiliations, physical torments and psychological abuse I am undergoing? To give you an example: I have had my bowels regimented. As I said earlier, I never had any problem with evacuating my bowels. Indeed, the daily opportunity provided me with much pleasure for its regularity. But the authorities here have seen fit to turn this innocent delight into a punishment with the purgatives they administer. As a result, all regularity has vanished and I am a martyr to cramps, looseness and a stinging sensation in the anus. My entire bowel is inflamed by being stimulated to open ten times a day, at odd moments when least expected. It is surely this that is adding to my weakness. I am being flayed from without and within.

I do not dare to open my eyes. I know the monsters are there, eager to reveal to me their ghastly deformities. Something is tapping on the window. I can hear a step in the corridor. The door handle is turning, the door is opening, the wind rushes in and on it the smell of dead animals. I keep my eyes tightly shut until I can bear the uncertainty no longer. My overalls have gone, my chef's hat and my utensils. My *batterie de cuisine* is to be forged into instruments of torture. A voice repeats: 'A cook, possessed, has grown into a ravening beast, biting his comrades and himself for food.' A man is circling my room touching the pieces of furniture as he circles, taking a single bite out of each object, swallowing before continuing his tour. I once saw a bird hit a telephone wire and fall to the ground dead. Minutes later it flew away with an alien soul in its poor body. This gives me hope.

I spot someone familiar I cannot identify dining off red mullet, toadstools in cream, grouse with orange sauce, stuffed artichoke hearts, a herb salad, a Grand Marnier *bombe*, Ventadour cheese and a plate of cherries. I cannot make out the wines she has chosen. She is dining alone, savouring each mouthful with eyes half drooped.

Before me images of scenes long past enacted, repeated again and again like a refrain from a cheap song. With his books to hand Carême coaches me through trout and all appropriate sauces, ptarmigans shielded with vine leaves, romaine and cress salad with walnut oil. But I loathe the very sight of food. I cannot taste my dishes. To sustain myself I shall need nothing more than the *soupe maigre* Carême invented for the Pontiff.

Seated in a semicircle on rexine-covered chairs, the women over eighty wait. They are dressed warmly in several layers of cardigans, felt slippers and woolly head-gear. (I am reminded of little wizened filberts in their shells.) Beside each is a small pile of belongings. I do not like to stare. I know they are biding their time before taking the last journey and are accompanied only by what they can remember: letters fastened with ribbons, sealed with a dried rose; a musty, moth-eaten fur tippet; a battered saucepan without its lid; a china dog without its tail; folded (and ironed) brown paper and little balls of carefully wound, used string; a rubber hot-water bottle; a braid of hair; half-bottles of tablets and linctus; half-squeezed tubes of ointment. The eyes of these women are empty, as if they had already died. One or two stand waiting in the corner with dunces' hats perched on their woolly hoods. Their faces express the dull bewilderment of the sick in mind. I notice some have their shoes on the wrong feet. Young men pass between them and force gnarled, arthritic hands on to their members. The women do as they are told while gazing into childhood, recalling the horses standing under the rain, their members hanging from their bellies, long, black and wet like hosepipes.

There is a foul stench coming from the shock-shop: burning wire and shit. (The sweet scent of *grande cuisine* turns to the sour stench of shit.) I follow my nose. Men and women are being slapped on to tables as far as the eye can make out. Their teeth are removed, replaced with rubber gags. Electrodes are being strapped to their temples. The pillows placed at the small of their backs do nothing to ease the shuddering jolts as they stiffen and fall back, their heads striking the leather, their distended, deformed bodies spitting out body waste.

'God save the fucking Queen!' At last the electrodes are being unbuckled from the sides of their heads and the wires unplugged.

'God save the fucking Queen!' The men nearest to me

90

have their eyes fixed on me. They are groaning in pain. 'God save the fucking Queen!' As the trapdoor opens to swallow them they shout in unison: 'Your turn next for electronic crucifixion!'

A line of naked blind moves slowly by. I cannot tell whether they are men or women; they are ranged so closely one behind the other they appear like a roll of corrugated paper. I see only one side – arm, leg and half-face, identical to the arm, leg and half-face in front and behind. There is an incalculable number, an unmeasurable stream of emaciated creatures, parchment in colour, soundlessly making their way. But where to?

I ask myself whether their nakedness gives them a dignity, or whether it robs them of it. I recall having read somewhere that for a woman to undress in front of a blind stranger is an insult of a particularly blatant kind, negating his existence. But are these blind people not being spared?

One of their number is taken aside. A man excavates her cavities with a pumping action before depositing his waste. I know she is being infected. I see his slimy juices at his mouth, nose and sex. Now he risks choking her. No words leave her mouth, only vomit.

Am I being dreamed into madness?

I flee. But I cannot ignore other threats and admonitions, other sounds near and far. The bruising sound of women shrieking is inescapable. Are they shrieking in the ecstasy of congress or the pain of separation?

A steady outburst from a fractured sewer emits things dangerous, disgusting, unjust and doleful. But I do not respond as I should. Something in me is past caring. My inanition has voided response.

Everything that ever entered this building must have excreted before it died. Now starving blind dwarfs, all mouth and claws, pick their way through the ordure of mice, birds and flies and feed one another with dried morsels of excrement and rotted flesh. They urinate from their temples into their fellows' ears. They grunt and they roar but softly, for they are very small. And when they need to rest they sit back to back chewing the lice from their own bodies. Those singled out to die of thirst are being stacked on shelves. Twelve inches separates the shelf below from the one above. They are stacked thirty-six high. I can see that some with greater life-force than others are struggling to drink the liquid waste from those above.

Were I to encounter something beautiful and harmonious, would I recognize it and respond? Surely I used not to be like this? I am almost certain of that. They do say the emotional vein is identical in every individual; all that varies is the thickness of the shell which this vein must penetrate. Sabine's was lithic. Has she made me in her image?

What blab is this about vice and vertu?
Evil propels me and the reform of evil propels me;
I stand indifferent.

Is it a million years ago that *my* matter cooled off?
A blizzard of gulls flies past the window: white on white. For the time being I elude my shadow. It has been pursuing me relentlessly, giving rise to a certain anxiety as to its intentions. I thought I might win it to my side by suggesting it went to spy on the ravishing young woman on my behalf. Surely I cannot be made responsible for the misdemeanours of my shadow?

I think ceaselessly about the young woman. In and out of my mind she slips on the gentlest of waves. She has started to replace all else. I float on a lake of thought about her; she and I become as indistinguishable as the water that gushes from the mountains and idles towards the sea. At the confluence, as of two streams, she is me and I am her. Will this bring retribution?

Yes. Immediately. A man is ordering a woman to sit astride him and drag his member through his fly. In a hurry. No time to take off his trousers. No time to take off her undergarment. Up rise his buttocks, down he drives himself into her. 'Come on! Show some spirit!' He falls back no sooner than started, face pouring sweat. He pushes her off, ordering her to 'Get me something to drink!'

What a joyless routine; skin against skin. A rhythmless pounding. No way to pass a desolate afternoon. Men do not make themselves good for women. I cannot think it can be comfortable for a woman to have a man atop of her, heavily crushing her breasts, only to leave her more unsatisfied than when she started out, then have him demanding other consummations. Roll, mount, cover, strike, release: a machine on automatic pilot. Is it for this? To be drilled, excavated and filled with viscous secretions that women remain faithful? Are they not aware that men can do as well without them? That in their absence they plunder furniture to arouse themselves, rub their members against the plush of drapes, the silk of cushions, squeeze into juicy melons and penetrate sheep? Or use one another with a chair-leg, a clenched fist and a toothless smile?

Savages rape women and kill and eat men. They rape men and kill and eat women. A starving man will suck food from the cunt of his mother. It is the madhouse of consumption: take, take, take. Ingest. Ingest. And at the moment of the most extreme deprivation, the screams are identical, interchangeable, horrific.

I have been devoured by women. Both by Aunt and Sabine. Devoured. And in order to keep me on the go they filled me with their particular need of me. I am a 'replaced person'. Now it is my turn. A woman, but not

93

the young woman, beckons. She has her arms outstretched. She wants to take me in but I shall refuse her. 'You can't fool me!' But she continues to beckon. She must be reading my thoughts, for she warns: 'Don't you dare call me a dish, a peach or your honey-bun. I am no edible commodity.' I do not argue. She is not a rich dish, nothing but a bread-and-butter woman. I laugh soundlessly, 'My navel is no oasis where men and camels come to drink. My stomach no sheaf of corn. My pudenda no orchard inlaid with an alabaster fountain. From East and West men come to take their pleasure, and with it mine. It is no consolation to be mere nourishment.'

I am filled with shame. I look up at her and accept the fig she offers. The white juice runs down my cheek, the semen from the swollen dark sack of seed runs to the corners of my mouth. This is sweet nectar. I reflect on her gesture, her offering. I am being generously received. In gratitude I give her what I can: 'Carême did not like fish to taste of thyme, bay, mace, clove or pepper but of fish. And so he always cooked fish in a little salted water and never made combinations of fish and meat. I take this to heart when I am at work. When I dress a *carpe à la Chambord* I remember "Here we have no more larding, no pigeons, no sweetbreads, no *foie gras*, no cockscombs and kidneys but a succulent ragout appropriate to this scale, with accompaniments and clusters of fish and truffles, nothing fatty . . . a harmony of tastes . . . no fancy platters, no overflowing abundance".' (My master eradicated all the ancient vices from French cooking.)

This woman has not eradicated the traditional vices of her sex from her behaviour. Nor is she rare and inaccessible. She will not do for me. I am hungry for what is exquisite, exotic and recherché, like a peasant child arrested only by a vision of the Holy Mother.

My mastery of cookery, my understanding of gastronomy, have gained me the special qualifications for the appreciation of women. My tactic will be to stalk the one I really desire with patience, avoiding all display of eagerness and over-excitement. I shall allow my ear the extended pleasure of her voice, my eye the lingering fascination of her beauty, my nose the intense intoxication of her odour. Only then shall I serve Priapus. But once I have satisfied my appetite, will it be assuaged for all time or will it demand repeated gratification? A fusion of the body is not, all said and done, of the mind. The beautiful young woman I desire belongs to another. I should be able to enjoy something, even someone in particular, without wanting to possess it. Being unable to deny oneself appropriation is the chronic symptom of collectorists. Many of my customers were thus diseased. They indulged their obsession with mansions for the display and storage of priceless medieval musical instruments, Sèvres porcelain, weaponry, blue teddy bears and historic golf balls. The richest among them employed special servants they sent to be trained in theft, to steal from museums all over the world. Although unable to display their ill-gotten gains (they had to keep them under lock and key in windowless strong-rooms designed for the purpose), although these items went unremarked and therefore unadmired and uncoveted, the collectors experienced utter gratification through the peculiar sensation possession gave them. Such men eat with the same passion. They are gluttons.

Sabine despised them and disparaged them tartly. (I have always been frightened of tongue-lashings.) But she took inordinate pride in the fact that to dine supremely well they were obliged to eat at Les Coteaux. No other establishment could touch the hem of our skirt, she would say. And they would pay whatever the price. Sometimes I did wonder whether my dear master would have wanted

95

me to labour for such as these. His was the aristocratic world. The lowest to which he sank – and this for only a very short period – was when he was employed by the Prince Regent and obliged to serve dark-brown gravies to be poured over and drown his exquisite raw materials and perfectly crafted preparations. But for whom would Carême have wished me to work? England could not provide me with a Talleyrand, a Tsar Alexander I, a Louis XVII – only property speculators, Lloyd's underwriters, bankers, politicians, pop stars, stockbrokers.

Perhaps the surge in my groin will open up a future of my own making. When I think back to Sabine, I recall an ice-box preserving within a self unknown, and not one I wished to pursue to its quarry. For whereas Sabine allowed herself to be penetrated physically occasionally (duty came before desire and outweighed it, I imagine), she never allowed herself to be penetrated psychologically or emotionally. It was this that rendered love-making rather joyless. Sabine's sexuality was like her courtesy, rooted in indifference. I remember even now the sound of her hysterical laughter when she told me a story about a woman whose passionate love for her husband was such that she wanted to eat him. (She murdered him and salted him against a hard winter.)

Thoughts of the young woman, on the other hand, arouse in me a kitchen-heat. In the eye of my mind I have already seized her in my arms. But to take her precipitately would be to deprive myself of the joy of savouring her. I know this. And, I wonder, would hunger once satisfied prove difficult, even impossible to reactivate? Hunger assuaged leaves no trace. Only the glutton desires a four-course meal after rising from an excellent dinner. Should the young woman prove as difficult to achieve as my liberty, I might die of passion. Would deprivation revive me? Supposing she submits too eagerly,

too readily? Do I want us to make love together knowing that we shall experience it separately, as we should
all else in life? Is it not a terrible corruption to be naked,
attached and alone together, yet utterly divided? A de-
ceit of nature? And now the discomfort of unsatisfied
lust is burning me. A torment of unappeased hunger gnaws
me. My obsession is leading me to an even deeper sense
of loneliness than that which has been my detestable
companion since my arrival at the Hollenhof.

Is this the grave? Is this the penitentiary and torture
the ante-chamber of the grave? I hear continuous noise. I
see naked men, some hung over crosses others impaled
on them. All are blindfolded. They are being questioned
and whether they answer or remain silent they are being
told 'You lie!' 'Answer me! You lie!' 'No, I do not!' 'There
you are, you see: you lie! Bastard. Unclean vermin. Rapers
of women, abusers of children!' And separating the cheeks
of their buttocks, warders in white coats ram their fists
into the victims' mouths and anuses. The superintendent
and his wife look on.

I stand back. I do not wish to be noticed. The torture-
chamber is the ever-present threat of terrible punishment
for something they know I have done – some misdemean-
our I have committed – but I do not.

An observer is disappearing into an ante-room with a
large bunch of keys dangling at her hip. I feel myself
impelled to follow her. She sits down on a piano-stool,
winds it up and down to find the height that suits her,
places a sheet of music on the rest and starts to play. No
sound emerges. I am hardly surprised: the interior of the
piano, an old one, has been 'drawn' like a fowl for the
pot, its strings and felts thrown out with the detritus I
narrowly escaped being thrown out with myself.

Who is to say that I am not dead, that I exist only in
the minds of my tormentors who have incarcerated me

and threaten me just because I think about the young woman? Is it not they who have robbed me of my energy to escape? Or is it that I do not really want to go back to what is familiar, to Les Coteaux and to Sabine? And yet there is nowhere else I long to be. My exile, and with it my discomfort, isolation and disorientation, does not engender in me a future I wish to attain, only a present dissatifaction I wish to allay.

Each time I allow myself the pleasure of thoughts of the young woman, they are interrupted by the sight of something aberrant. Even now it is happening. A man is rolling towards me, his head between his thighs, his sex in his mouth. His legs are flung over his shoulders and he has tumbled to my side in a state of euphoria. I turn away. I am in an empty room. Something taps on the locked window. The handle of the door turns. The door opens. The stench of the dead rushes in on the wind. I am thrust into the corridor where walking drunks hug the walls to let the tumbler pass as they make their way towards the first drink of the day. I smell their vomit, their urine and their alcohol. They hold their shaky heads high with a single thought: how to get a drink. Crawling with nits, stubble-faced, lank, long-haired, toothless, wrinkled and weak bladdered, they go on their way. One stoops to retrieve a dog-end from the floor. Others follow suit, lighting their finds with split matches. Homelessness and hunger mean nothing to them any more. They are accustomed to both and to their running noses, coughed-up phlegm and scabrous skin. I watch them drinking against the wall of the public lavatory.

I should change my clothes before I approach the young woman. But which of the dozen shirts Sabine packed for me should I choose? I cannot take decisions here. I usually wear what will go well with what Sabine has chosen for herself. On the rare occasions when I feel an obstinate desire to wear something that might clash with her outfit, Sabine is able to persuade me out of my preference.

It is not only when I allow myself thoughts of the young woman that something sexually aberrant confronts me. I have only to dwell on my hunger for love, for what I was denied in my youth, for the most horrible examples of gluttony to appear. I believe this place must be where love and fulfilment are eliminated. It is the seat of indifference, where warnings are administered as the ultimate deterrent.

Waves of dispossessed, shipwrecked men are breaking up in the foyer. It is high tide. I back against the wall: I must avoid being washed out when the tide turns. But I do not want to linger among these half-dead men whose bodies are twitching like headless chickens, whose dirty words infest my hair, obstruct my breathing and obscure my vision. I shall need to take great care to avoid the detritus of family life deposited on the beach. I am anxious not to be grazed and risk infections from the motorless machines, broken tables and chairs and soiled clothing.

In the distance I can see the young woman on a rocking-horse galloping leisurely through the spume, swishing its tail.

Does this corridor have no end? And why are all the doors numbered fifty-five? Can it be that the function of each of the spaces behind the doors is the same: to ingest the redundant contents of dead men's houses? To pulp the tuneless piano, the springless three-piece suite, the blunted knives, handleless suitcases, chipped cups, cracked vases, torn sheets, sodden boxes, foxed pictures, smashed window-panes? Fifty-five is the name given to the Graveyard of Things. If I am not careful to move swiftly out of the path that this identically, neatly compacted

99

detritus the size and volume of a family car is taking, I shall be crushed. I am pretty sure that somewhere along the corridor this method of disposal is being applied to guests who resist treatment.

I shall deprive the authorities of the satisfaction of packing me for disposal. I shall dispose of myself. This decision gives me a delicious sensation, a strange feeling, strange because I have never felt it before. I believe it is the sensation of authority. Now that I am free of Sabine (or is it that Sabine is free of me?), I shall starve myself. By taking the decision to stop eating I shall properly renounce the past. Everything I used to take in was a mere substitute for what it was I wanted and needed. I shall void it all and what does not come away at once will eventually dissolve. I shall drain away, like time, part of the process of decomposition. They do say that the most spiritual of human beings can live on air. Indeed to do so is said to assure an ecstatic experience: a drunken frenzy of delight. My body has never brought me this satisfaction in the past. (Thoughts of the young woman are pressing against my mind.)

It has not taken long. My body is starting to disintegrate. I am curious to know whether my spirit will notice its disappearance. My flesh is torn. Strands of red arteries and blue veins dangle from my arms and legs, leaving a pool of congealed blood smelling of iron at my feet. My stomach is a vile mess, whey-coloured against my plum-red liver. Both are pushing through the skin of my torso on their way to the open, where they lie like tumours, dripping with puss. Shall I be able to choose what to dispose of and what to retain? If the evacuation of my organs proves too precipitate, I shall simply swallow back what I need. Ice has formed on my body hair and tightened round me with the force of guy ropes in an involuntary effort to contain what is left inside me. I

100

am taking my destiny upon myself! Sabine would never have permitted this.

Now that I have found a way to compose and decompose myself at will, I shall continue to conceal Carême within me, but I shall stop evacuating him as I used to. I see now how wrongly I used my master, devouring his words only to void them. I was under the domination of a lust to please that I could not control, hungry as I was for my master's directions to guarantee me a position I would otherwise never have attained. Not with my own ideas. To have claimed Carême for myself was a deplorable thing to do. I am filled with remorse. By eating his words they became less than his. Sabine's ultimate immorality was to have encouraged this in the first place, and then to have discouraged it for the wrong reason. It was not that she understood I ill-used my master. It was not this that made her intervene. She wanted me to invent for reasons of fashion, novelty and approbation. I shall store Carême inside me secretly and leave Sabine for ever on the outside.

When I was working I knew who I was. But I was misinformed. I was no more than the embodiment of what Sabine required. Now that I am not working, I am no longer her invention. I neither nourish my own nor anyone else's illusions. I am nobody's invention, not even my own. It would be, I imagine, of some satisfaction to me were I to discover an identity. My first inclination is to inquire of someone where I might find one, but no one here is the least interested in me. They will not so much as listen to me or stop to pass the time of day. Sometimes I think they do not even notice me, because if they are lingering near me they never turn to face me.

I have a vague idea that were I to take a succession of decisions to put things right either for myself or for those I have seen abused, I might discover myself.

101

I am drawn to the young woman not only for her exceptional beauty of form but because I can see her inner self is patient and concerned. I cannot prove this to myself but I sense it to be so. I find this reassuring. It leads me to believe I might go to her and ask her who I am and what I am doing here, witnessing the most frightful goings-on that I had always known existed but had made every effort to avoid.

I shall do my best to proceed logically, that is to say I shall search methodically for the young woman and for the least uncomfortable circumstances. I have never caught sight of her near the torture-chamber. She probably confines herself to a corner of tranquillity. I shall furnish her tranquillity with objects of beauty, harmonious sounds, fragrance and matters of interest. I shall make love to her.

I am so impatient to be with her. And once with her I shall be impatient to be part of her. I am going to enter into a conspiracy to turn something of this hell into a paradise. For fifty-five years I walked the quays without embarking, for fear of the limitlessness of the seas. I kept my eyes shut against the demons eager to devour me. No longer. Having opened my eyes, I feel ready to embark. But I wonder: am I quite ready to put these plans into operation? Have I prepared the ground adequately? I know I must not hurry unduly. Sabine was always precipitate. When she set the sweet-pea seeds in her window-boxes with a stake beside each seedling, no sooner had the plant reached four or five inches than she was worrying it to twine. No matter what lengths she went to, the little plants twined only when they were good and ready. Not before. From my own experience, I can vouch for the same being true of the preparation of food. The processes cannot and must not be hurried. And so I am repeating to myself: NO hurry! NO hurry!

I wish I had applied that ordinance in the past and taken time for all of life, to look and listen, to consider and reflect. Only now does it occur to me how much I might have enjoyed being a customer, sitting in a café with a glass of wine and a book, the murmur of voices about me, no obligation to perform. To have had time. Yet this idea comes to me only now, at a moment when it is least realizable. All my life I have worked excessively to keep at bay thoughts that would otherwise have paralysed me. Since being here my demons have taken shape, my fears have been made incarnate. I cannot escape them, yet I fancy I see how they might have been avoided.

It is a state of mind that gives rise to reflection. Those who have no need to work keep themselves busy *entertaining* themselves. Time abused is a dereliction of the imagination.

Am I conscious or unconscious? Before I came here I kept to a routine. I could tell the hour by where I was and what I was doing. Time and place identified me. But here time seems to bend and twist, making what seems to have happened a projection of what may or will happen, as if everything were a warning. And the present is merely hypothetical. I do not know whether it was yesterday or a week ago that I arrived at the Hollenhof, for night and day do not slide seamlessly towards and away from one another for their existence. I do not think I am unconscious, for in that state time does not exist at all. I must be either less or more conscious than I was. Could it be that I am dreaming? Or am I being dreamt?

And what of my size? I have encountered dwarfs so small I could have swallowed any one of them whole, like a pea. I have brushed against giants so huge that any one of them might have imprisoned me in an armpit. But now uncertainty nags me. Do *I* shrink and expand?

103

Were those I took for dwarfs and giants of normal proportions?

I am suffering inner devastation as if locusts had laid waste to me. There is no point to my outer husk, for it has nothing to enclose. I am made void and inactive. Am I here to be replenished or punished? If to be nourished, where is the feast? If to be punished, where is the court where I would have the right to be heard and my prosecutors the obligation to listen?

Time has stopped. That is not to say the clocks have stopped. No! They tick away, their pendulums swinging irregularly, their faces all telling different times. Were I to muster the energy to follow some sort of routine, it would prove impossible. Routine requires strict adherence to a timetable. Indeed, time is a pseudonym for life itself. And I am doing time. I always have been doing time.

I miss timetables. I used to collect them as a child. (And at school I learnt my times-tables early and had no problem committing them to memory.) As an adult I made my own: one for every day of the week so that I would always know precisely where I should be at every moment, where my staff should be, and how much time to allow for each of my dishes. I found security in timetables.

A troupe of men bound in canvas strait-jackets has appeared. They move in slow motion, as one, in a monstrous pain they cannot express. Their jackets crack like pistol-shots, for they have had icy water thrown over them and been left in the open to freeze. These men will never remonstrate or write on walls. Their ideas have been frozen out of them.

The man who used to walk about putting grass in his

pockets is suffering untold frustration here, where there is none. He is clutching his hands in hopelessness. (There is no vegetation here, not so much as a moss or a lichen. What was Sabine thinking of?) I want to tell him that if he no longer sought grass he might be an entirely happy man, like the woman beside him at the table. She has before her pieces of white, orange and blue felts. She is cutting out a circle of white and is tinting the edges brown and crimping them with her fingers. At the centre of the white she places a wadge of cotton wool and over it she sews a small circle of orange felt. Now she takes a large piece of blue felt and cuts out a plate-sized circle. On the circle she places her fried egg. Before settling to eat, she ties a napkin round her neck and reaches for the salt. 'Light is like scissors,' I hear her say, 'the way it cuts things up.' And now she looks at me accusingly, 'Why do I wear a snake-skin in my hat? Because it is a charm against diseases of the head, that's why.' Is she real or have I improvised her? For she has vanished. (I believe she has been here for forty-five years. She stole a pint of milk.)

Are these mad people invading me, taking me over, making me think their thoughts?

At least that woman knows how to occupy herself. I don't. I have not been told how and there are no helpful notices. Or have I been told and forgotten? I thought Sabine sent me here because of my interest in Parflavium. She said it grew here, above the snow-line. The little quantity I managed to germinate in the deep-freeze was not enough for my culinary purposes, I never succeeded in producing a strong root stock and the leaves of my plants were too faintly perfumed. Sabine sent me here to replenish my stock. She said I would find a root or two. But I can't get out into the open. I am stuck here watching skeletons warming themselves beside icy radiators.

105

Who are they, these people? Who were they when they had flesh on their bones? They sit talking to one another like men and women thrown together on a cruise.

Sabine must have been in league with the attendants. She almost certainly would have had to sign papers giving authorization for them to do with me as they saw fit. But is it likely that in such a place as this I could learn to become inventive? Could not Sabine have foreseen that I was more likely to become inert? I have seen where the files are kept at the reception desk, where the particulars of each guest are noted and the orders for their treatment promulgated. Did Sabine subscribe to my file, I wonder? I have seen men in suits accompanied by prim secretaries codifying the treatment to be meted out to each person. And beside the stacks of files I have seen the wires extracted from the compacted pianos hanging beside dirty-white hooded cassocks and the torches that will burn bright when the virtuous are pursued to their death.

I am shaking uncontrollably. Since the beginning they came, the multitudes. Now they are gone, leaving behind a waste land and of themselves, something no more corporeal than the most fugitive odour. The dead await burial. I must climb over a heap of body bags that have slipped from a pile stacked against the wall. Here rot the men and women who did not respond to treatment. I must burn them or their putrefying flesh will burst out and the whole corridor will be awash in their black, stinking fluids.

I dreamed of Sabine with a black dog at the crossroads. I could not make out the dog's tail but to its left I noticed the churchyard and knew the dog was hell-bent on digging out the dead.

My mind is stiff with the shapes of death and dying. I cannot shut out the death-rattle in the hills.

Predators, shady operators, omnipotent invaders, persecutors threaten. I must take the greatest care not to identify the object of my desire, for fear of retribution. But in my heart I know that unless I identify her and include the flickering behind my mind, I shall achieve nothing. Such contending feelings are paralysing me. My tongue is locked. I am inert as stone, cold as the cold at the bottom of a well. Who is my most deadly enemy? Until I am absolutely sure, how can I defend myself?

What means this celluloid man who sings on two notes 'gone down, gone away, gone mad'?

I do not read. I hardly bother to throw my ear on voices telling their stories. I have no desire for food and drink. I am at the crossroads of action and inaction, of will and motivelessness. Survival does not attract me, nor yet does non-survival. Often I think I must be dead (existent only in the mind of my master, hurt at his own abandonment), destined to sit here for all eternity, subsisting on the lees of conversation, watching horrors I am powerless to correct. This lassitude is the visible part of moral turpitude. No bell could summon me; no instruction rouse me. I stare at the wall, but the wall merely absorbs my stare, returns me nothing. I had imagined that were I to concentrate long enough on it, it would reveal its secrets. But as soon as I start to wonder what is behind it, I grow bored with my own curiosity and form no image.

I want nothing. Once, generated by habit, I knew what was required of me and rose to that expectation. Here, now, alone and without work, I do not know what to do or who I am. I used to accept habit as being adequate a recompense for happiness. Now I have neither.

The Hollenhof is oddly empty. Even the air is thin. Down the corridor, into the foyer, through the dining-room not a sound, not an object stirs. The cushions on

107

the chairs retain the shapes of people once sitting against them; the ashtrays are full; the magazines are askew on the little tables. Everyone has gone. The curtain has come down on the final act.

I feel so alone I talk to myself. Failing to hear what I am saying, I shout. But I cannot understand my own vehemence. I address the chairs. I reassure them that I sympathize with the weight they have had to bear. I turn to address the foyer: 'I understand how empty you must feel!' A mad woman singing sweetly would be reassuring.

Somewhere in this castle of sadness and humiliation, where the horrors man has contrived to nourish his spleen and the price of unloving prevail, the young woman exists. Does she share my love-longing? Has she had to endure the sights and sounds I have had to endure? Has she remained as apathetic as I when faced with the sight of unidentifiable men and women shivering in gelid cells on concrete floors, wrapped in sour blankets, rotting from their gangrenous feet up? Has she intervened when the guards swing these unfortunates round their heads, splattering the walls with their innards?

Past, present and future are simultaneous and actual, a vast canvas, a narrative that can be grasped by the eye and taken into the mind and understood instantaneously.

Among the dead in their icy dormitories, I am filled with shame. It is shame that fills the ever-widening gap between what I see and think and the action I fail to take. Sometimes I cannot find the words to describe what I see. Aphasia *is* the gap. My worry is that I may vanish before leaving an account of what I have seen happen to others and what I myself have personally endured. To have lost my voice, to have no voice, is the worst of punishments. Despite my never having wished to lie, to misinform or to dissemble, my voice has been taken from me because, I think, I have aimed at not feeling.

My situation here is made unbearable because I am able to recall the past, a place and time at which undifferentiated terrors dogged me and Sabine ruled my life: where I practised to become perfect at un-feeling. Here, without Sabine, I am lost. Here, where my terrors have taken shape, I am powerless to confront them. There are no keys to the doors and I cannot escape. And were there keys, I might not have the strength to turn them. I am acclimatized to coercion.

On the rare occasions I succeed in finding my room, I try to gather my fugitive thoughts by naming the objects there. My room is no more than four paces long. It contains a bed, table, chair and wardrobe. The window is barred and overlooks a well. The door is either locked to exclude me or handleless to confine me. I have no practical use for any of the objects. I am forbidden pencil and paper, so I do not sit and write at the table. (Some people, I believe, have been led to write on the walls with their excrement for want of these little necessities.) I do not sit down; I am too restless and so the chair is of no use to me. The window mocks me for the view it had best obscure. As for the wardrobe, it is a thing of such mystery and potential threat, I prefer to pretend it does not exist. (Pregnancy has always offended me.) The looking-glass aims to convey much more than I wish to know, and I dare not lie down on the bed for fear of falling asleep. All this furniture is mere sculpture to me, its purpose simply to displace space. The worst of it is that I can recall the *douceur* that once it brought: views over beautiful countryside from a window, tables groaning under the weight of exquisite food, the warmth and comfort of a bed turned small craft lulling me on still waters, transporting me to places of enchantment.

I find myself torn between the twin feelings of safety and confinement. I am persuaded the executioner is in wait and that stillness will bring him out, so I must keep moving. I pace the room: four steps north, four south. (There are poets who compose this way. I believe the rhythm they achieve generates the fluidity they need for their inspiration.) At first this pacing, being limited to eight steps, makes me dizzy. But as I persist, I notice that my feelings of safety on the one hand and that of passing from one confinement to the next on the other separate, as if claiming to belong to two different people (for how could one person accommodate such contradictory impressions?), and I start to consider the proposition that I *am* two people. I had felt this duality particularly keenly when torn between turning right or left at the top of the stairs in an effort to regain my room. It seems I contain Siamese twins who coexisted in the past without need to bother me and only now combine to sabotage me. What-to-do and Fail-to-do are asserting their identities.

I continue to pace and while I do so I consider all those things that send men mad: eating lobster after dinner, disappointed love, too much study, a blow on the head, lightning, loss of fortune. Lust. And forthwith my thoughts turn to the young woman and my intentions towards her.

There is nothing to distinguish the outside from the inside. The sky hurls hail stones at the windows, the wind drums rain at the door; cold clings to the furniture; the saliva at the corners of my mouth freezes.

A flock of birds, white and quiet, pass. They move their wings in unison. It is as if they were one sole bird, a unity of fowl in a single body. Never before has unity felt a more desirable state of being.

I need to regenerate myself, find a self of some worth, and a direction. There are no answers here and that being the case questions are superfluous. I must stop questioning. There will be no explanations, no illumination. Only the evidence of things unseen. An ominous silence

110

has consumed the past. I have lost it. I feel I may have arrived at the very centre of my life or a new beginning.

Even here where the price of unlove prevails, the young woman exists. I have seen her with my own eyes. Sight of her reminds me that I have never experienced ecstasy. I have read about it, heard talk of it, made mention of it and watched an approach to it on the screen. But never known it. If I can attract the young woman to me, if I can seduce her, I know I can be assured of a delirium of love and a derangement of passion. And that that state of being will transform the ordinary and ensure against the raging hunger and thirst of the void. If I am to be possessed, and it would seem that possession is my fate – whether by Sabine or the demons that terrorize me – I choose to be possessed by the young woman. And if I am to be too weary to take action against my demons, it must be the heart's ease of completion that hinders me rather than the weakness anxiety imposes.

PART THREE

The lover knocks at the door of the Beloved, and a voice replies from within: 'Who's there?' 'It is I,' he said; and the voice replied: 'There is no room for thee and me in this house.' And the door remained shut. Then the lover retired to the desert, and fasted and prayed in solitude. After a year he came back, and knocked once more at the door. Once more the voice asked: 'Who is there?' He replied: 'It is thyself.' And the door opened.

Anon

I have passed into the open, into a landscape of an infinitely repeating, unpunctuated phrase. Massive blocks of ice are ranged in couples as if reflected in mirrors, stretching into illimitability. Above, the sky is clear as polished glass. The light is blinding and so I close my eyes. When I open them I see that a fog is building to roll over the ice-blocks like some massive, lusting beast.

Now the wind is hissing like a snake, curling in and out of whatever is in its path, carrying away the odour of decay instilled in the sacks of mouldering men and women. Snow is gently falling as silently as silence itself, obedient to some law that is its alone. Beneath my feet the earth is stiff under its white shroud. I bow my head in reverence.

It is not for nothing that we speak of the dead of winter. And I am aware of the shears of fate that approach my own life-thread. Yet I do not imagine it will be a physical malady that mows me down. These icy circumstances that exist between consciousness and unconsciousness are barren and present a sullen uniformity, but also something tough and impervious to infection. And so I can be glad to be outside, stepping across the snow varnished lightly with ice, with all about me dazzling, clean and wholesome, sculpted by the wind, far from the opinion-houses of the world.

115

I have caught sight of the young woman. She is seated, reading. She is dressed in the palest yellow voile, which matches her hair. She is peaceful, absorbed and obviously content to be where she finds herself.

My thoughts lie, as long they have lain, like paving-stones, one grey and recognizable leading to another indistinguishable from the former. Fearful certainties. But I notice now between the cracks mysterious *un*certainties, heavy with energy, bubbling with life. It is possible, no more than possible, that there resides within me more than I know. I caught sight of a solemn madman in the foyer. He had a shaved head, goitred eyes and stubble all over his face and neck. He was neglect itself. He stopped suddenly in his tracks in front of a rose bush. He carefully removed a thorn from a stem and pricked his finger. He raised this bleeding finger to his eyes and I saw his face transform itself into a smile. I knew he was feeling the uncustomary possibility of life.

She lay like a dry winter leaf. I felt that if I did not catch her up in my arms, she would be blown away by the breeze. She roused herself, said she had been out, had walked she did not know how far and found a mountain lake. Had located it, she said, for the reeds that poked through the snow. 'Frozen stiff as glass' she said, 'quite beautiful.' Her eyes shone, her hair smelt of hay, her body moved like music. Can that which awakens my heart satisfy it? I asked myself.

In. Out. In. Out. Inside. Outside. I am uncertain. I am possessed. She comes to me ten thousand times ten thousand, caresses me, hypnotizes me, makes my desire her own.

I am poised between forgetfulness and remembrance at that confluence nearest death and consummate pleasure. All I want is to stop thinking. To stop thinking, particularly, of the process of penetration: to forget that the whole

116

majesty of sexual fulfilment is no more than a rush of blood. (I have seen too much of blood.) And to forget the language of this so-called love-making: the stuffing of birds, the picking and the nibbling of juicy pieces, of things coming to the boil, of grilling the beloved to come clean, of time for a quick one; not to mention the sucking and the licking, the tasting and the appreciation of forbidden fruit, the satisfaction of ripe, fragrant flesh and the simmering passion that leads to consummation – and all the other words phrased by my customers and used impartially in their pursuit of food and women. ('*Toute la nature que nous avons sous les yeux est mangeante et mangée. Les proies s'entiernordent.*')

I sense misgivings too vague for words. And terrors so palpable I want to avoid their expression: she will die; I shall be alone. 'It is best,' I insist, 'for us to die at once.' (So final, so unassailable. I weep.)

I take the pickaxe and hack open the iron bolts and sever the chains and padlocks. I pull the boards and bars off the windows, throw open the windows and let in the air. I take a crowbar and pulverize the doors. I watch as the carpet of slime and excrement dissolves, gathering up and taking with it the stench. The struggle is no longer against impossible odds.

The space I have made for the young woman is clean and tidy. It has no unlit corners. It is fragrant. It wants for nothing to make us comfortable. We fuse. My body, which felt only pain at its depths and at its surface the barbs of contempt, which turned against itself and disintegrated, is now as sensitively tuned and elegant as an eighteenth-century stringed instrument. And even when I walk, I do so in time to her words. I am becoming what I should be.

'I wonder . . . what thou and I did, till we loved.'

'I shall love you until the snows melt.' She is lying

117

coiled in my arms. We love in the dark and in the light. I leave myself and enter her and it is good. I know myself; my mind is emptied of all but peace and my body tingles with expectation before trembling on waves of satisfaction. I am replete.

I rise and go to the window. My heart leaps to see the beauty of the scene: a soundless, endless white with just her breathing to remind me. And I dwell for a moment on the thought that that which looks so perfect can create circumstances that are deadly. Under this avalanche there must be animals frozen to death. Under these frozen streams there must be fish preserved like flies in amber. I have not seen a single live insect, heard the song of a bird, caught sight of the paw marks of a mountain hare. And I have seen what the unknown forces are capable of when mindful to create havoc: ice-blocks half a mile across falling from the brumous sky, winds that gather whole mountains in their grasp, enduring cold. And I have witnessed the whole diversity of man's inhumanity.

'Where are you going?' I ask her as she prepares herself to leave, believing that were she to tell me I might control the event. She does not answer but drifts away. I know that I must stay put, so that when she returns she will experience the room as she did the first time, here where untarnished thoughts and desire reside.

This is the emotional life I never had. I have created a sort of paradise: an uninterrupted cycle of passion leading to pleasure that arouses passion. In the past, I avoided ardour for fear it might overwhelm me. Now I am ready for it.

She is by my side. 'You are dreaming me,' she says. 'It will be worse for you when on waking you find you have lost me.' I answer her with kisses. The scent of the datura is making me drowsy. She and I lose ourselves together, drift to the other side of a drugged sleep.

A persistent, irritating noise that I cannot name invades my pleasure. It disturbs me mentally. Physically, it nudges and pushes me so that I float upwards. Images of a chef's toque, a Sabatier knife set, savarin mould, fish-kettle, braising-pan and stock-pot float with me, accompanied by a sort of serenity I feel may endure. My kitchen re-calls itself to me with nostalgia, and I feel a generosity towards a past I cannot bring to mind.

The noise takes shape to become a sound, that of a klaxon, the one that sounded when the coach swept into the forecourt of the Hollenhof.

I find myself standing at the reception desk. I am the last of the guests who travelled on the coach to enter the inn. The manager is pushing the visitors' book towards me, asking me to sign the register. It is 14th May. The manager has his back to the wall of files, his arm raised to summon a bellboy. He hands the boy a key and tells him to show me to room fifty-five.

I let the boy go ahead with my case. I follow him as far as the stairs but there I pause to look out of the long, thin windows that rise from the foyer to the top floor.

I look forward on a land subdued. Junket white. Hori-zontal but not flat: a white darkness sinking from the sky and rising from the ground, swirled about by a wind that is gathering plates of snow-crust in its grip and hurling them against the inn.